Possession

EXPLICITLY YOURS ◆ BOOK ONE

JESSICA HAWKINS

© 2014 JESSICA HAWKINS
www.JESSICAHAWKINS.net

Editing by Elizabeth London Editing
Proofreading by Tracy Seybold
Cover Design © OkayCreations.
Cover Photo © shutterstock.com/g/kiuikson

Possession (EXPLICITLY YOURS SERIES 1)

This book is a work of fiction. Names, characters, places, and incidents either are products of the author's imagination or are used fictitiously. Any resemblance to actual persons, living or dead, events, or locales is entirely coincidental.

ISBN: 0997869119
ISBN-13: 978-0-9978691-1-8

TITLES BY
JESSICA HAWKINS

LEARN MORE AT JESSICAHAWKINS.NET/BOOKS

SLIP OF THE TONGUE
THE FIRST TASTE
YOURS TO BARE

THE CITYSCAPE SERIES
COME UNDONE
COME ALIVE
COME TOGETHER

EXPLICITLY YOURS SERIES
POSSESSION
DOMINATION
PROVOCATION
OBSESSION

STRICTLY OFF LIMITS

Chapter One

Each night started with the flip of a switch. Hey Joe's neon OPEN sign flickered and hummed to life. Lola's watch read 5:59 P.M., but time had no place on the Sunset Strip. Johnny wiped down the wraparound bar with the efficiency of someone who did it more often than he brushed his own teeth.

"Opening at goddamn six o'clock," Quartz said, shuffling in. "You ever heard some people like to drink their lunch?"

"But if we opened earlier, you wouldn't get to say that every night," Lola said.

Quartz's whiskey on the rocks already sat in front of his stool. "Bad enough you're going to cut me off in eight hours. When's Mitch going to wake up and open his bar at a decent hour?"

"Don't think he'll be getting to that," Johnny muttered. "Your tab's hit its max, Quartz. Need you to pay that tonight."

"But if I did, you'd never get to say that."

"I'm serious." Johnny kept the whiskey in his hand, ready to refill Quartz's glass. "You see anybody walking through the door? This isn't back in the day. Look around."

Quartz made a point of twisting on his seat. "Looks like the same old trough I've been drinking out of since '67."

"The point is, you want a bar to come to every night, need to help keep us in business."

Lola shook her head quickly at Johnny.

"What?" Johnny asked, leaving the bottle on the bar to serve a customer. "They'll find out at some point."

Lola ducked under the hatch and came up behind the bar. "Don't listen to him," she said to Quartz, taking Johnny's rag and picking up where he left off.

Quartz put the rest of his drink back with a jerk of his head. "Never do. Figured out years ago that your boyfriend's ponytail holder is cutting off the circulation to his brain."

"He gets crabby when business is slow," Lola said. "Mitch's been breathing down his neck about bad sales."

Two more regulars came in and took their seats next to Quartz. Lola served them and stood back as they grumbled about their wives, bosses and neighbors. At least, those were the typical topics. She wasn't actually listening because she was watching Johnny at the opposite end of the bar. For the third night in a row, he checked the bulbs on a string of busted Christmas lights that'd been up for nine months.

"Why don't you just buy new lights?" Lola asked.

"Because these ones are fine, babe. There's only one broken bulb. I just need to find it." The lights were even smaller in his sizeable hands. He raised his brows at her. "You going to trade me in for a newer model the day you figure out my one flaw?"

Lola smiled. "After nine years, you must keep it pretty well hidden, whatever it is."

"Care to take a guess?"

"Definitely not ego," she said and winked at Quartz when he snorted.

Lola looked up as Veronica breezed through the front door and dumped her purse on the bar.

"Vero—" Johnny started.

"Bus was behind schedule." She shrugged off her denim jacket.

"Where's your car?" Lola asked.

"In the shop again."

"Lola was supposed to work on some flyers tonight, but she had to open the bar for you."

"Well, she can go now." Vero grinned as if it were the brightest idea. She threw the jacket over her purse and tied an apron around her waist. "Think I can handle this rowdy group on my own."

There were only five customers. Veronica had been working at Hey Joe even longer than Johnny. At forty-two, her sarcasm was worse than ever.

Lola went in back and sat at Mitch's computer. She didn't know much about design, but cash was too tight to hire a professional. The bar only had three shows scheduled that month anyway, so she made the flyers herself. She did a good enough job that before Mitch had started talking about selling the place, he'd suggested she give the happy-hour menu a go.

After an hour, Johnny dropped a plastic takeout bag in front of her. "One chicken Caesar salad for the in-house marketing team."

"I'm not hungry," she said, looking back at the screen. She was hungry, just not for her usual. If she said that, though, Johnny would feel bad and go get her something else.

Johnny picked up a flyer from the printer tray. "Nice. I like this font."

"It's recommended for bars and restaurants," she said. "I researched it."

He set the paper down. "You almost finished? It's picking up out there."

She stood and stretched her arms. "I'll be right out."

She put the salad in the refrigerator and stole a couple bites of someone's pad thai noodles. Before she'd even reached the front, she heard car engines revving from outside.

Quartz swiveled around on his barstool. "They trying to wake the dead?"

"Nah. Just get some attention," Johnny said. "Ignore them."

Fumes seeped through the door, clouding the room. Lola spent five or more nights a week at Hey Joe, the place she considered her second home. The staff and the patrons were her family. So when a lone beer drinker in the corner booth glared at her, she went to see what the commotion was about.

It was dark out. People roamed down the Strip's sidewalk. The owner of an electric-blue Subaru, who couldn't have been much older than eighteen, honked at her.

"We got customers inside," she called over the racket. "Take it somewhere else."

He hit the gas again. Parallel parked behind him was a black Nissan with red rims and a matching spoiler. The driver turned his music up so loud the sidewalk vibrated.

Lola went to the curb. With a rag from her apron pocket, she waved away exhaust fumes. It took one well-placed, swift kick of her Converse to put a dent in the Subaru's fender. "I said—"

"What the—?"

"Get the fuck lost!"

The driver jumped out and came around the hood toward her. Lola braced herself for an argument, but he stopped mid-step and looked up.

"You heard the lady," Johnny said from behind her. "Don't make me call your mommy."

"Look what she did to my car." The kid pointed at the dent. "That's a brand-new paint job."

"She's done worse to men twice your size," Johnny said. Some men by the door snickered.

"But—"

"Look, kid," Johnny said. "Something you should know about this little stretch of the Strip—we don't call the cops. We handle our own business."

The boy flipped them off with both hands but returned to his car.

Johnny squeezed Lola's shoulders. "Can't go around kicking people's cars, babe."

She glanced back at him. "He started it."

Even with affection in his brown, gold-flecked eyes, the look he gave her was louder than any words.

"Aw, come on," Lola said. "I'm not the one who threatened to *handle* him."

"Why do you say it like that?" He tucked a loose strand of his long hair behind his ear and half smiled. "Think I can't take a couple punks?"

"Oh, I know you could. I also know that you, Jonathan Pace, are all talk."

Johnny winked. "Not when it comes to my lady."

With a kiss on the back of her head, he left Lola standing at the curb. She slung the towel over her shoulder. The two cars took the pavement in a fury of screech and burn, and what followed was a rare moment of silence. Sunset Strip was always busy, but every year the crowd at Hey Joe thinned a little more.

Lola turned to go back inside. Everyone had cleared the sidewalk except one man, who was watching her. He stood by the door with a hip slightly cocked and his long arms straight at his sides, as if he'd been passing by and hadn't meant to stop. Even in the dark, she was struck by his movie-star good looks. He could've wandered over from a movie premiere on Hollywood Boulevard, except that he was too buttoned up.

"You lost?" she asked.

He straightened his back. "What gives you that impression?"

"If you're looking for happy hour," she said, pointing west noncommittally, "try a few blocks down."

"There's no happy hour here?" He checked the lit, orange sign on the roof. "At Hey Joe?"

"Not the kind you're looking for."

He touched the red knot of his tie. "It's the suit, isn't it? I look out of place."

She moved closer, pulled by the deep lull of his voice. The LED beer logos in the window turned the lingering smoke multi-colored. His deep-set eyes were dark, his jaw abrupt in all its angles. She had to tilt her head back to look up at him.

His attractiveness sank its teeth in her, more obvious with every passing second. "Not just the suit."

"What then?" He ran his fingers through his stiff, rust-colored hair. He had so much of it that the gesture made some strands stand on end. "That better?"

It was that he was too much—his green, almond-shaped, watchful eyes, and his tall, straight back. He didn't match the carefree laughs and imperfect postures of the people inside the bar. He turned them into commoners, with their round faces, round eyes, round bellies. It was that until that moment, she'd thought she knew what it meant to get butterflies.

But she couldn't say those things. "We just don't see a lot of suits at this end."

"You work here?" he asked.

Lola stuck her hands in the pockets of her apron. "Not like I wear this thing to make a fashion statement."

His loud laugh almost startled her. When he stopped, it echoed. He looked from her neck down, everywhere and all at once, as if he might reach out and touch her. His perusal made her feel exposed, and she was glad her apron subdued the cropped T-shirt and leather pants underneath it.

"You really did a number on that car," he said, his eyes back at her face.

Lola didn't embarrass easily, but there was no denying the sudden warmth in her cheeks. Wherever this man came from, people didn't kick cars there. "You must think I'm a real class act."

"Doesn't matter what I think."

"I guess that's a yes then." She shrugged, because he was right—he was a stranger. She did things like that all the time in front of customers, new and old. Then again, none of them had ever given her butterflies.

He turned his head toward the door so his profile, as straight and clean as his suit, was backlit by the sign. A face as handsome as his almost seemed predatorily arranged to disarm prey. "That was your boyfriend?"

"Who, Johnny?"

He looked back at her. "Ponytail and Zeppelin T-shirt. Big guy."

She shifted on her feet. "How do you know he's not my husband?"

"You aren't wearing a ring."

She balled her hands, which were still in her apron. The man stared at her longer than was appropriate, but she wasn't ready to look away. That was why she had to. "I should get back to work."

He nodded. "So should I."

She glanced around the block. There weren't any offices nearby.

Before she could ask, he said, "I was actually on my way in for a drink with some colleagues. I'm here on business."

"Here?" she asked. "This bar?"

He turned and pulled open the door. "This very one. After you, Miss…?"

Light slivered onto the sidewalk. From the bar came a soundtrack of snapping pool balls, glass bottoms on tabletops, men arguing. "Lola," she said, then amended, "Lola Winters" because he looked like a man who dealt in last names.

"Lola." He smiled up to his dusky-green eyes. "Beau Olivier. Nice to meet you."

She didn't move right away. She liked the closeness of him. "Sounds French, but you don't."

"I'm not. My father was," he said. "I grew up here."

"Was?"

"He passed away."

"I'm sorry," Lola said.

"It was a long time ago. *C'est la vie.*"

"C'est la vie," she repeated.

He looked at her expectantly. For a moment, she'd forgotten they were about to go inside. She cleared her throat and walked through the door. Hey Joe's interior was booths mutilated by cigarette burns older than Lola, and black and muddied-white checkered linoleum flooring. A neon-pink mud flap girl watched over the crowd from behind the stage. They were things Lola only thought about once in a while when she considered reupholstering, replacing or removing them. But she thought about them then.

"What can I get you?" she asked over her shoulder as she walked.

"Scotch, neat."

"Preference?"

"Macallan if you've got it."

She stooped behind the bar. "That isn't on special, Beau," she teased.

He smiled again. "I like the way you say my name."

"Yeah, well. So does Johnny."

Beau joined two other men at the bar—the ones who'd snickered on the sidewalk earlier. They were younger than Beau, younger than Lola even, in T-shirts and flannels, jeans and sneakers. She wouldn't have looked twice at them if they'd come in without Beau.

Lola made his drink, glancing at him from under her lashes. He'd loosened his tie. She noticed things about him she hadn't in the dark—the early shadow of stubble forming on his cleft chin, fine lines around his eyes, dimples that hugged his smile like parentheses. He'd called Johnny big, but Beau likely surpassed him in height.

Beau walked back to her end of the bar. She gave him his Scotch.

"Is it just me, or does alcohol taste better on a Friday?" he asked.

"See those guys?" She nodded at Quartz and the others posted in their usual spot. "Tastes the same every day of the week to them." She watched them as if looking through a window into her life. It didn't matter the day, their conversations ran a loop of the same topics. That kind of thing was standard around there. "Bottomless glasses, arguing about bullshit. I still don't know how they function day to day when they're here drinking four, five nights a week."

She turned back to Beau. He'd been staring at her profile and flinched when she caught him, but he didn't look away. He lowered his drink on the bar.

"What?" she asked, busying her hands by filling the sink with dirty glasses.

"Nothing."

"Not nothing." She turned on the faucet and squeezed dish soap into the water. "I've seen that look before."

"I don't doubt that."

She glanced up. "Looks like that lead to trouble."

"Probably. I'm not good at keeping my opinion to myself, though."

She paused. Warm water rose up her forearms. Instinct told her to ignore the comment. She'd done a good job of staying out of trouble since coming to Hey Joe. It'd been a while since anyone besides Johnny had looked at her that way, though. With some hesitation, she asked, "What's your opinion?"

He squinted at her. "You move around this bar like you've been doing it for years. But something doesn't quite click. I'm wondering how you got here."

"That's easy," she said. "On two legs."

"Then what keeps you here?"

They stared at each other. He didn't look as though he expected an answer, and that was good. She wasn't going to give him one—it was none of his business.

"You think you have me figured out in ten minutes?" Lola asked.

"That's ten minutes longer than it takes me for most people." Beau kept his eyes on her face. "And that has my attention."

"Is it hard to get your attention?"

"It's harder to keep it," he said, without even a threat in his voice that he might take his attention away. Even though neither of them moved, it was as if they were getting closer and closer. "But you, Lola, you're—"

"We're low on change," Johnny said, turning the corner from the back office. "Can you do a bank run Monday?"

Lola plunged her hands deeper into the hot water and fumbled for the sponge. "Sure," she said and wiped her brow with her forearm. "Yeah. I have to make the deposit anyway."

Johnny looked from Lola to Beau.

"This is Beau," she said. "Apparently my little show out front made him thirsty."

Johnny nodded once and shook Beau's hand. "Johnny. Welcome."

"This your bar?"

"Nah. I just manage it with Lola."

"She's modest," he said. "She didn't say she was a manager."

"*Assistant* manager to my *boyfriend*." She looked at Beau's empty glass. "Guess you needed that drink. Another?"

Beau reached inside his jacket and took out his wallet. "Looks like it'll be one of those nights. Let me guess…cash only?"

Lola nodded and refilled his drink.

He put some bills on the bar and gestured toward the men he'd arrived with. "For our first round. Everything they order goes on my tab."

Johnny blatantly stared at the cash-stuffed, dark leather wallet in Beau's hand.

"Do they work for you?" Lola asked.

"Not yet. But I want to show them a good time."

"So you brought them here?" she asked, raising her eyebrows. Hey Joe could definitely be a good time, but it was a lot of other things too, like rough around the edges.

"This is the type of place where they're comfortable," Beau said. "Which is what I'm after. A colleague suggested it, said it's been around a while."

"Only fifty-three years," Johnny said. "It's practically a landmark."

"Longer than I realized," Beau said. "What makes it a landmark?"

"It was the place to be in the sixties and seventies," Johnny said. "Live music drew everyone from bikers and hipsters to actors and movie producers."

"I guess that's why the Hendrix reference."

Johnny nodded. "The owner's dad saw him perform 'Hey Joe' here on the Strip late one night for a small crowd. Apparently it was so magical he named the bar after it. Man, I would've fucking loved to have seen that. Not that I was even born yet, but still."

Beau looked at the microphone on the empty stage. "What happened to the music?"

Johnny shrugged and leaned his hip against the counter. "The club went pay for play in the eighties when Mitch took over. Bands didn't like that, and we lost our cred. Fans followed the music elsewhere."

"How's business now?" Beau asked.

"It's all right. We get acts in here some weekends, but nothing to write home about."

Beau shrugged. "You never know. These days, it's all about the comeback."

"That would be great, but it's not pulling in half of what it used to," Johnny said, shaking his head. "Can't afford to keep the doors open."

Beau glanced up around the bar. "Well, considering its history, and if it's still got some name recognition, he should have no problem selling the place."

"That's the plan. Sell or shut it down."

"Johnny," Lola warned.

"Secret's practically out, babe." Johnny looked at Quartz and the other guys. "It's just those dummies down there who know nothing about anything."

"I take it they won't be too thrilled," Beau said.

"Some of them have been coming here since opening day," Johnny said. "No, they won't like it."

"That's a shame." Beau picked up his drink. "I should get back to work. If you'll excuse me."

He left Johnny and Lola to get a table with the other two men.

"What're you thinking?" Johnny asked, nudging Lola's shin with his shoe.

She looked from Beau's table back to Johnny. "Just that it's been a while since I heard you talk about music like that. When's the last time you and I went to a real concert?"

Johnny closed one eye as he thought. "Years. Concerts usually happen at night. We don't get a lot of nights off together."

"We should ask Mitch for one soon. They can survive one night without either of us."

Johnny kissed Lola on the forehead. "I would, but he's got a lot on his plate right now. Let's see how things work out these next few weeks."

"Oh, I remember the last time we went to a show that wasn't here," Lola said. "Beastie Boys, Hollywood Bowl." She smiled as the memory played out on Johnny's face. "And then…"

"That's right." He paused. "The night we had that huge argument."

Lola nodded and leaned toward him. "Which then became the night of the drunken angry sex." Her heart kicked up a notch. "What would you say to an encore? A bottle of tequila, a show and you getting lucky?"

"An encore? We must not be thinking of the same night," Johnny said. "We both drank way too much. I don't even remember what we fought about, just that a table lamp paid the price."

"Me neither, but I do remember one of the best orgasms I've ever had," Lola said. Her ass throbbed. It wasn't the only time Johnny had spanked her, but it was the first and last time he'd done it like he'd meant it. It'd been like sleeping with a stranger after having the same partner for years.

Johnny shook his head. "I don't understand. You want us to have another blowout fight?"

She shrugged one shoulder. "Not fight. I just think a night out could be good for us."

"That's not something I want to recreate," he said, turning away. "But I promise, once things get sorted here, we'll do something for ourselves."

Lola frowned. That night had always stuck with her in a deranged, inexplicable way. There'd been something crackling in the air. She'd assumed the same was true for Johnny, but apparently he'd experienced something else—something entirely different.

Beau was heading back toward the bar, a slight swagger in his step. He didn't look as though he'd hesitate a moment before delivering a hard slap on her rear end. Lola's breath caught.

"We'll take another round," he said, leaning his elbows on the bar. "Might as well keep them coming."

Lola grabbed a glass before Johnny could, eager for the distraction.

"You guys play?" Beau asked. He gestured to a cup of darts against the back wall.

"Yep," Johnny said. "My girl's queen of the bull's eye."

"Is she?" Beau grinned. "Up for a game, Lola?"

"Why don't you play with one of your friends?" she asked. She handed Beau his drink and pointed at the end of the bar. "Or the locals will take anyone on. When they're drunk enough, you can clean them out."

Beau lifted his glass to his mouth, shaking his head. "No challenge in that. I only go up against those who play to win."

Johnny wiped his hands on a rag and nodded over at Lola. "Then you want this one. Got a bit of a competitive streak."

Lola was wary about spending too much time around Beau. They were already hedging on dangerous territory. "Sorry, but I've got customers."

"It's all right, go ahead," Johnny said, taking the drink in Lola's hand. "I'll get these to the table."

She hesitated. "Are you sure?"

"Why not? Go. Have fun."

She shrugged. "Okay. If the boss says so."

"If you think I believe I'm really your boss, you're fooling yourself," he joked. "We both know it's just a title."

She laughed but stopped abruptly at the way Beau stared at her—as though he'd forgotten Johnny was even there.

"What should we play for?" she asked. She stuck a hand in her apron, pulled out a few dollars she'd made in tips and showed them to him. "It's all I've got on me."

"I'm thinking slightly more than that," he said.

"Like what?" she asked.

"How about a hundred bucks?"

"That's a little steep. I'm confident, but I'm not stupid."

"The higher the stakes, the better the game," Beau said. "Not worth playing if you don't have something to lose."

"It's fine, Lo," Johnny interjected. "I got you covered."

A hundred dollars wasn't chump change for Lola and Johnny, but she had a feeling it was for the man standing in front of her, waiting to play. His tie was silk, and his suit custom—nothing from the rack. Lola knew enough to tell the difference.

She came out from behind the bar, and Johnny passed her the darts. When she went to take them, though, he wouldn't let go. Their eyes met. He told her with a look that, just like Lola, he smelled the money on this man.

The dartboard was on the opposite side of the bar, against one of the dark, wood-paneled walls. She and Beau walked by the regulars, under the dated, medieval-style chandelier and by some yellowed Polaroids of rowdy patrons.

At the toe line, a strip of curling duct tape, Beau held one hand out. "Ladies first," he invited.

He didn't know much about her if he thought she was a lady—and didn't know much about darts if he thought that was how you decided who threw first—but Lola kept her mouth shut and took her place. Her dart just missed the triple twenty. She aimed the second one a little higher and landed it.

"Impressive," Beau said. "Where'd you learn to play?"

"Johnny taught me when we first started dating. Before long I was better than him." She threw the last one. "Some people just pick it up easier."

"Or maybe you're like me. I never take my eye off the target." His dart bounced off the wire. "Sometimes I miss, but I never miss twice." He threw again, this time hitting the center.

He got quiet for his last throw. She watched him, the constriction of his neck when he swallowed, the tautness of his jaw while he concentrated. If he was this self-possessed and powerful looking during a light-hearted game, she guessed he'd be a force everywhere else.

"Where'd you say you work?" she asked him.

"I didn't."

"What do you do?"

He threw his dart, but neither of them watched where it landed. "I'm a founding partner of a venture capital firm downtown."

"Those guys you're with don't look like colleagues."

"They own a tech startup I'm thinking of investing in. I like to take my time getting to know the people behind the project before I make any decisions."

"Isn't that kind of thing normally done in a conference room or over a golf game?"

He smiled. "Sometimes it's a golf game. Sometimes it's a trip to Vegas. For these guys, a local watering hole's where they're most comfortable."

"What about you, though?" she asked. "Are you comfortable here?"

"It's not my first choice." He looked at her closely. "But I don't mind a change in scenery now and then. And this is definitely a departure from my usual thing."

Lola took her spot at the duct tape and threw. "I can't tell if that's a compliment or not."

"It is. Take the women who work for me, for instance. They're all blonde. Even the ones with dark hair look blonde. I don't know how they do that."

"Well, this is L.A.," Lola said. She retrieved her darts from the board and passed them to him.

He didn't move right away, except to turn a dart over in his hand. "You don't see any with hair like yours."

"Mine?" Hers was more of a mane, black and thick as the day was long. Straight too—she got that from her dad. One of her few memories from before he'd left was a woman stopping them on the street to say Lola was her dad's spitting image. "What's that supposed to mean?"

"That color—pitch black. It reminds me of the night. Unpredictable. Smooth, but a little wild. No end, no beginning, like midnight. But then your skin," he continued, shaking his head as if in wonder, "white like the moon." He laughed abruptly and took his Scotch from the nearby high-top table where he'd set it. "Well.

I've been known to get a little romantic when I drink, but this has to be a new level."

"It's nice," she said without thinking. Her palms were sweating. Come to think of it, the bar seemed warmer than usual. "This place isn't exactly known for romance."

"What's it known for, Lola?"

She blinked several times as she thought. "It used to be…electric. Regulars insist you could see this block from space, all lit up in neon lights. Hear it too."

"Still a lot of neon here," he said.

"True. It takes more than some neon signs to make a place electric, though. Lately people gawk like we're some kind of relic. Problem is, we're still here."

"Gawkers aren't good for business?"

"Not if they aren't spending. I keep telling Mitch we need to become relevant again, because we're really lacking new business. And when the tourists forget about us, we're in trouble." She took another turn. "So how come you don't know all this if you grew up in Los Angeles?"

"I know some of it. I've just never been big on nightlife."

"Why not?"

"I work a lot. In my twenties I was an employee by day and an entrepreneur by night."

"Building your firm? What's it called?"

"Bolt Ventures, but no, I'm referring to my first company," he said. "I went through a lot during those years, but it eventually paid off."

"Do you have hobbies?" she asked, arching an eyebrow. Before he could answer, she added, "Outside of work."

He blew out a laugh. "Some," he said. "Mostly it's just work, though."

"God, you must love what you do," she said and smiled. "I'm all for working hard, but it's nothing without some fun."

"Don't worry," he said evenly. "Because I work hard, I get to have fun too."

Her smile wavered wondering how a guy like Beau had fun. Johnny played guitar, but only for himself. A rock band in high school was the last time he'd performed publicly. Otherwise it was video games or tinkering with cars and bikes at the auto shop where his best friend was a mechanic.

Beau, on the other hand, wouldn't play an instrument. Not the guitar, anyway. She couldn't picture him with a gaming controller or a wrench in his hand either. He was tightly wound. If a man like him didn't loosen up once in a while, he'd snap.

Johnny didn't stress out often, but even he needed to unwind. A couple years back, Hey Joe's alcohol order had gotten mixed up right before the only bartender on duty called and quit. "At least he called," Lola had said, but Johnny wouldn't hear it. His parents had moved to Florida days before, and Lola's car—long gone, now—wouldn't start. Johnny's eyebrows had been so low on his forehead, she'd worried he'd scare off customers. With five minutes to open, Lola had taken him in the back and given him the blowjob of his life. He'd been fine after that.

Lola squinted at Beau. It'd been years since she'd thought of that. She definitely had sex on her mind tonight. Had Beau ever been blown in a seedy bar like this? Would it relax him? Turn him on? Would he find that...*fun?*

"I'm boring you," Beau said. "I never go on about myself this much. Either the Macallan's kicking in or you're too easy to talk to."

Lola was about to tell him to keep talking—she liked having a new voice in the bar. It didn't hurt that that voice was bottomless, as if it came from some untouched depths inside him. And steady, in a comforting way. She could listen to him all night. She shook the feeling off.

"So what'll you do if this place gets bought out?" he asked.

"I try not to think about it," Lola said. "It'd be hard on us. Johnny loves this place as if it were his own."

"And what about you?"

Over Beau's head were some photographs of the owner's dad with bands and customers who were long gone. "There's a lot of history here," she said, her eyes wandering over the pictures. "I'm closer to the people here than I am my own family."

"But you could see yourself doing something different," he guessed.

"Different?" It hadn't occurred to her. Johnny had been bartending for twelve years, and she'd been by his side for eight of them. They were a team. "The late-night scene can get old," she admitted. "I suppose if it were between moving to a different bar or trying something else, I'd maybe think about something else." Lola hadn't even known she'd be open to a change until she'd said it aloud. She'd assumed she and Johnny would always work together, but Johnny'd never do anything outside the nightlife industry.

"Something like…?" Beau asked.

She considered it a moment. "A restaurant would make sense, or a coffee shop. At least the hours would be better."

"So then serving food and drinks is your passion," Beau said.

She simultaneously laughed and scoffed. "I wouldn't go that far. I'm just being realistic about my options. They're limited without a college degree."

"You didn't go to school?"

"Dropped out my first semester." Lola mock-gasped with her fingers over her mouth. "Unheard of in your world, isn't it?"

"No." He frowned. "I didn't go to college either."

She cleared her throat. She hadn't expected that. Yet, he only said he'd started a business—not that it was successful. Maybe it wasn't. But there was his suit, the cut of it, the way it moved with him instead of against him. It turned his shoulders into two strong right angles with a large expanse in between.

If she pretended there were a bug, she could reach out and brush it away just to see if the fabric was smooth, scratchy or something else. And she could get an idea of what was underneath it.

"What'd you do before this?" Beau asked, oblivious to her wandering imagination.

"Before this? Nothing really. I've worked here since I was…" She almost couldn't finish the sentence. It was a lifetime ago now. In the eight years she'd been doing it, she couldn't pinpoint when she'd decided waiting tables would be her career. "Twenty-one," she finished. "That's how old I was when I started."

"So that would be, what?" Beau pretended to count to himself. "Two years ago? Three?"

"Nice try," she said as she laughed.

"I can't be that far off. You could pass for early twenties."

"Maybe compared to tonight's crowd. You and I might be the only ones under forty." She guessed at his age to see if he'd correct her, because he could very possibly *be* forty.

"Except for Johnny," Beau said.

"Obviously except for Johnny," Lola said quickly. He'd flustered her with the insinuation she'd forgotten about Johnny—because she had.

"You're a bit younger than me, though," Beau said, his voice light, teasing. "And I'm a bit older than you."

She wanted to ask by how much, but she just glanced at the floor. "Not a lot older, I don't think."

"The way you're smiling a little makes me think maybe you wouldn't mind an older man."

"Actually," Lola said, lifting her head, "I wouldn't know anything about that. Johnny's the oldest guy I've been with, and he's a few years older than me. And my guess is you're a few years older than him. And my other guess is, whether or not I'd mind an older man isn't really your business."

His eyes twinkled. "You're right. It was inappropriate to suggest you might. I'm sorry."

"I don't think you are." She turned away from the probing look on his face, more intimate now than it'd just been.

"I don't think you are, either," he said.

She paused, and against her better judgment, looked back. His cheeks were high and round, as though losing the fight against his smile. "Don't tell me you're forfeiting the game," he said.

"And give you the satisfaction? Never. I'm in it 'til the end."

"Then why are you walking away?"

"If I'm going to hang around you any longer, I'm going to need a drink for myself."

He put his hand in his pocket and stalked slowly toward her. No longer on the verge of smiling, he looked at her as though she were on display in a museum, some rare and amusing find.

She stood her ground, even when he came close enough that the tips of their feet almost touched. His eyes, their unusual oval shape and striking color—he narrowed them and frowned as if he were trying to read her but couldn't. He leaned in. He was going to kiss her right there in front of everyone. She had to move, push him—something. She looked at his mouth, his bottom lip slightly fuller, slightly pinker than the upper one.

26

"Are you going somewhere dangerous?" he asked.

She tried not to sound as breathless as the thought of kissing him made her feel. "What?"

He put his hand over hers, encompassing it in warmth. He turned it over. Instinctively, she opened her fingers to reveal a dart she hadn't realized she'd been gripping.

"I'll hold onto this—unless you think you'll need it for protection?" He took it and walked back a few steps. She wondered if she'd been wrong that he couldn't read her because of the way he grinned. It was as if he knew something about her she didn't.

Chapter Two

Once the OPEN sign was switched off each night and the doors locked, Hey Joe became something else. The pours went from standard to generous and the music from loud to easy. Familiar.

Veronica and Lola closed down behind the bar while Johnny and his friends surrounded the pool table, looking like some kind of biker gang. There were no motorcycles in the parking lot, though. Mark, Johnny's best friend, had traded his in kicking and screaming when his son was born, and the rest of them couldn't afford anything worth owning.

Outsiders weren't usually allowed after hours— Johnny's rule, not the owner's—yet somehow Beau had convinced the guys to let him in on a game of pool. Lola suspected that was because they never got a chance at winning real money when they played against one another. The men Beau arrived with had left hours earlier.

Lola turned the volume up a notch for The Doors. Veronica shook her hips back and forth. Her acrylic nails clinked against drink glasses as she dried them.

"I heard a rumor," Veronica said.

"Probably the same one I heard."

"Think we'll all get the boot when Mitch sells this place?"

Lola looked at Johnny as he lined up his shot, sank the ball and swaggered around the table. "I hope not," she said.

"Word is they're looking to develop this block of the Strip into something fancy. You see that juice bar they're putting in?"

"I saw it. Can you imagine bulldozing all this history? Vero, do you realize the fucking rock stars who've stood on that stage?"

Vero popped her gum, shaking her head. "Shit's not cool."

"They'd probably give us uniforms. You might have to wear a miniskirt."

Vero looked down at her Harley T-shirt and faded jeans. "The day I wear a miniskirt's the day I cut off my balls and serve them to my boss on a silver platter."

"You don't have balls, Vero."

"It's a saying," she said, rolling her eyes. She leaned a hand on the counter and nodded over at the pool game. "I don't know, maybe it wouldn't be such a bad thing if this place shut down. Not like Johnny can't find something else."

"But he's perfect here."

She smiled. "I know. That doesn't mean he can't

find good work somewhere else, though. And maybe you could do something with those flyers you're working on."

"You think so?" Lola asked.

"Why not? I remember when you first started you talked about going back to school."

"Yeah, I did," Lola said. "Kept putting it off and here I am years later."

"Happens all the time, but people do it. You could take a graphic design class or something."

"That's not a bad idea," Lola said. "I actually like the little bit I've taught myself."

"Yep," Vero said. "But take it from me, you have to do it now. If you get another waitressing gig, you'll get stuck again. Me and Johnny? We're in this scene for good. Nothing can hide a lifetime of smoking and the pretty little scar on my lip Freddy left me with. Johnny's got his rough edges too. You can still get out, though."

Lola chewed on her bottom lip. Once in a while, she thought about going back to school. Johnny didn't like change, though. Leaving the bar would mean no more waking up late in the morning together and lounging before work—coffee, talk shows, reading the *Times* while he strummed his guitar on their tiny patio. It would mean not driving home from work in the middle of the night, sometimes with her head in his lap when she was especially tired. It would mean leaving him behind in a way, telling him this life he loved wasn't quite enough for her.

"Everyone's living in the clouds tonight," Lola said softly, thinking of the similar conversation she'd just had with Beau. "There must be something in the air."

"Nah. It's just the liquor giving me loose lips," Vero said.

"Veronica," Lola scolded. "Johnny warned you about drinking on the job."

"You know how it is. I just need a taste every now and then. Anyway, you had a drink earlier."

"That was a special circumstance."

"Playing darts is a special circumstance?"

Lola pinned her with a look. "My aim gets sharper the more I loosen up."

"Oh, okay, sure." Veronica nodded her head high. "Keep your secret if you keep mine?"

Lola snickered. She rarely got to pull one over on Johnny. "Fine," she said. "Deal."

Vero stopped her gum smacking. "Girl, why don't you ever tell that slut to back off?"

Lola followed her nod to Amanda, one of the waitresses, as she smiled up at Johnny.

"You know why," Lola said. "She can flutter those lids until they fall off, Johnny's not dumb enough to touch that."

"Don't matter. Since she doesn't seem to have eyeballs, there're other ways to let her know he's your man."

"We have to work together," Lola said. "I don't want trouble. And Johnny puts her in her place when he needs to. Not that it does much good." Lola's gaze shifted to Beau, who stood with his pool cue planted on the ground. He was the only one not wearing something faded or leather.

"Handsome guy, isn't he?" Vero asked. "Out of the suit, that is."

Lola kept her eyes on him and shrugged one shoulder. "I don't mind the suit."

"Don't tell Johnny that. Probably never wore a suit in his life, not even to a funeral."

"I know," Lola said absentmindedly. "Maybe that's why I like it."

"Replace the suit with a cut and throw him on a bike, though? Fuck me. A face like that would put a serious dent in the pussy around here."

Beau caught them looking and raised his glass, his smile sweetly crooked.

"You didn't answer my question earlier," he said after she'd gotten herself a drink. They'd stopped playing darts and were standing close to each other at a high-top table.

"Which one?"

"I asked what you did before working here."

"Oh. Nothing really. There was high school, of course…"

"Of course." He grinned. "But you didn't work here until you were twenty-one, which leaves a few years in between. Maybe the answer to your quandary lies there."

Lola leaned toward him over the small table. The bar was busier now and the conversations more animated. She told herself it was to hear him better, but she was actually afraid of missing even one word. "And what quandary is that?"

"The one about what happens if Hey Joe goes under."

"Ah, that one." She picked at nothing on the table. "No, it won't answer that question."

"I'm pretty good at problem-solving," Beau said. "Try me."

Lola was unaware she even had a problem. A new idea to

explore, sure, but not a problem. She opened her mouth, about to tell him to mind his own business. She wasn't ashamed of her past, nor was she proud of it, but something about Beau made her wish there were nothing to tell at all. Instead, she gave him a version of the truth. "I did some things, met some people. I went through a stage where I partied a lot and crashed on friends' couches."

"That's vague," Beau said. "How much is a lot?"

"Too much."

"Is that why you dropped out of school?"

She nodded. "I blew my money on alcohol and going to see bands. Sometimes drugs too. I couldn't keep up with the tuition, but I'd been missing classes anyway."

Beau studied her. "How'd you end up here?"

"Johnny," she said right away. "He's the reason I got my life back together."

He cocked his head. "Really? Why?"

Lola picked up the darts from the table and backed away, suddenly disgusted with herself for discussing this with a stranger. Johnny never judged her, never made her feel ashamed. She was by his side every night because he'd believed in her without having any reason to. She didn't need to explain herself to Beau. "Let's finish the game," she said.

Beau lowered his drink, but held Lola's gaze a little longer than necessary as they exchanged a private moment. He turned back to the pool table.

"He seems especially interested in you," Vero said.

The memory scattered along with their moment. Maybe it hadn't been as private as Lola had thought. She wiped her forehead with the back of her hand and got back to cleaning. "Sure," she said, "if overworked barmaid is his type."

After a few minutes there was a cheer from the table, and Johnny high-fived Quartz. He set the cue in its rack and walked over to Lola. "Won back the money you lost at darts and then some," he said, leaning over the bar for a kiss.

"Good job, babe."

"I'd better quit before I do any more damage," Beau said from behind Johnny.

Johnny turned around. "You taking off?"

"Once I settle my tab. I might be a little short after that game, though. ATM?"

Johnny pointed toward the back wall and watched Beau walk away. "Lo," he said under his breath. "See if you can convince him to come back. Maybe bring some of his moneybag friends."

"What's it matter?" Lola asked warily. "The bar's closing anyway."

"Nothing's set in stone, babe. It's a long shot, but those business types love to slum it up once in a while. Go now, while he's alone."

Lola's stomach knotted just thinking about it. It didn't feel right, but Johnny rarely asked her for much. "What am I supposed to say?"

"Just be cute, flirt a little." Johnny eyed Beau then did a double take at Lola. "Not too much, though." He printed out Beau's tab and handed it to her in a black, vinyl sleeve. "Bring him his bill and ask when he's coming back."

Lola rolled her eyes but took the bill even though she doubted she could flirt with someone who always had the upper hand. If Beau wanted flirting, he'd be doing it. She approached him as he was taking his money from the ATM.

"Hey," she said with a smile. "Thanks for the game tonight. It's been a while since I lost."

He raised an eyebrow as he counted out some bills. "You're thanking me for that?"

Lola averted her eyes from the money to be polite. "It's good for my ego."

He smiled, returned his wallet to his jacket and nodded at her hands. "Then you're welcome. Is that my check?"

She handed it to him. He slid money into the fold without looking at the total and gave it back to her. "A little extra for the great service."

She took it. "Johnny says you can come back any time you want." She fidgeted with the folder. Tonight had been something different from the usual because of Beau. Most nights she and Johnny had the same dinner, talked about what the bar needed to improve, saw the same faces. She wanted Beau to come back too, but if he knew that, he might get the wrong idea. "I think he likes you," she added.

His eyes narrowed on her as if he was trying to figure something out. "Does he?" he asked. "What about you, Lola? Do you like me?"

She fumbled for an answer. "Do I like you?" she repeated, stalling. Heat crept up her neck. That was twice in one night he'd made her blush. "Sure. I enjoyed talking to you."

He threw back his head and laughed. "That's it?"

"Yes," she said. "Should there be more?"

"I thought there might be." He looked past her a moment, then his eyes shifted back. He cleared his throat. "I'm an early riser, especially when I have to work in the morning. Meaning, not much could keep me out this late."

"Well, I'm glad you had a good time," she said.

"What I'm trying to say is, you're the reason I stayed." He stepped a little closer. "Any other night I would've left with the people I came with."

"But I'm so boring." She said it with a smile because smiling and making a stupid joke seemed like the only safe response to what he was implying.

"You're the least boring person I've met in a while," Beau said, "and it goes against my nature to bite my tongue. I like you, Lola. I think you already figured that out, though."

"Let me guess. Subtlety goes against your nature too. How many women have fallen for that?"

"Have you seen me even look in another woman's direction tonight?"

She hadn't. Once Vero'd brought up Amanda, Lola had been curious to see if Beau would talk to her. Amanda wasn't a bad-looking girl, but Lola didn't worry about her because Johnny just wasn't a cheater. He didn't have it in him.

But if Beau was looking to take home a sure thing, and he had a penchant for a bar girl he could flaunt his wealth for, Amanda was it. Yet earlier, when Amanda had smiled at him across the pool table, he hadn't even acknowledged her.

"That excuse is too convenient," Beau continued. "You're trying to cheapen our attraction by suggesting I'd take anyone home."

Attraction. To be drawn to him—to want to feel even closer to him when they were standing right next to each other. It fit them too perfectly, and that sent a chill down her spine. "I think it's best we end this conversation here," she said, keenly aware that her boyfriend was mere feet behind her.

"So I'm wrong then," Beau said. He stood far enough from her that their conversation wouldn't have appeared intimate. But each time he spoke, it was as if he removed another layer of her clothing, and now she was too close to being exposed. "I'm wrong that this attraction is one-sided?"

Lola glanced over her shoulder. Johnny was saying goodnight to his friends at the door. She looked back and almost told Beau he wasn't wrong, that it wasn't one-sided, just to see what he'd say. Flirting with him gave her a thrill she hadn't felt in so long. "I'm sorry if I gave you the wrong impression," she said instead. "Johnny and I have been together a long time, and we're happy."

"That's not what I asked," Beau said. "How you feel about him is one thing. Whether you're attracted to me is another."

"I'm not," Lola said firmly. She could've admitted the truth to any other man, because she was confident in her love for Johnny, but Beau wasn't any other man by a mile. Her gut told her the truth was a risk she couldn't afford to take.

Lola went to leave but stopped when she opened the bill holder. There was a stack of twenties. She counted three hundred dollars, but his total was ninety-seven.

She stuck only enough in her apron pocket to cover the bill. "This is too much," she said, turning back to Beau. "I can't accept this."

He hadn't moved. He raised his eyebrows slowly. "It's called a tip."

"No, I know, but it's too much. The tip is double the bill, and I didn't do anything out of the ordinary."

"So, let me get this straight," he said levelly. "You won't even accept a generous tip?"

He almost seemed angry. She almost *felt* angry. That much money wasn't a tip—it was suggestive. It turned their harmless, flirtatious exchange into something sordid and cheap.

She took the cash out and thrust it at him. "Please. I'm not comfortable taking this."

His mouth was closed, but his jaw worked back and forth. She didn't recognize the look in his eyes, but it cooled any warmth that'd been growing between them. "Fine," he said, taking the money from her. "I don't believe I've ever had a tip returned to me, but I suppose there's a first time for everything."

"Thank you," she said. She walked away with her fingers gripping the empty folder.

"Well?" Johnny asked as she approached the bar. "How'd it go?"

She shot him a look. She was too annoyed to answer, but she couldn't have even if she'd wanted to because Beau was right behind her.

"This scene has been a nice change from what I'm used to," Beau said. "You've really got a good thing going here."

"Like Lola said, I hope you'll tell your friends," Johnny said. "We could use the business."

Beau looked pointedly at Lola. She hadn't mentioned telling his friends. "I will," Beau said. "Even though I kind of like having it as my secret."

Lola held his gaze, willing herself to think of anything but *attraction*. She was failing.

Nobody spoke for a few moments and Vero, who'd been busy closing out the register, chimed in. "Can I get you some water or something before you go?" she asked Beau.

"You mentioned the owner's looking to sell," he responded, glancing between the three of them.

"That's right," Johnny answered. He leaned back against the bar and crossed his arms. "Why? You know someone who might be interested? We'd really like to find an owner who wants to keep Hey Joe as it is."

"Every struggling business wants that," Beau said. "They want to keep doing what they're doing without sacrificing a single thing, but they want it to magically become profitable."

"This place has the history to back it up," Lola said defensively. "We believe in it."

"And I admire that." Beau turned to Vero. "Veronica, is it? Would you give the three of us a moment?"

Vero winked. "Sure thing, baby."

"I'll go with you," Lola said. "Give the boys a chance to talk."

"I wouldn't," Beau said. The warning in his voice kept Lola's feet glued where they were. "This concerns you."

Vero left, swaying her hips especially wide on her way to the backroom.

"Have you thought about buying this place?" Beau asked them.

"Have *I*?" Johnny set his palms on the edge behind him and sighed. "Owning a bar is the idea one day, but not this one. Even if it is on the decline—well, you're a businessman, you know. The brand has a solid reputation. It's already got the foundation for success, just needs the right owner."

"You're worried about the price."

"Nope," Johnny said. "If I were worried about it, that'd mean I had a chance in hell of getting the money."

"I have the money to buy it." Beau paused. "I can *give* you the money to buy it."

Lola's heart had already gotten a workout that night thanks to Beau, but right then it thudded once and painfully hard—as if it'd been running, come to a screeching halt and smacked into her ribcage. Everything clicked for her. This was their answer. This was why Beau had been so interested in her and the bar. He saw an opportunity, but she saw their first glimmer of hope in a while.

"You mean like an investor?" Johnny asked.

"No," he said. "I'm talking about a one-time

payment to buy the business and the liquor license outright. You wouldn't owe me a dime of your profits."

Johnny pushed off the bar and stood up straight. "I'm listening."

Beau squinted at Johnny for a few seconds, but it looked to Lola as if he was somewhere else. "There's a catch, of course—"

"I think you got the wrong idea about us," Lola said suddenly. At first glimpse it'd sounded like an answer, but as Beau's eyes darkened and his tone dropped, she didn't want to hear the next thing out of his mouth. "We may not have much, but we're honest people. We do things by the book around here."

"Let the man talk, Lo," Johnny said.

She was too surprised by that to utter anything else. She and Johnny *did* do things by the book, especially Johnny—there was no reason to dismiss her.

"It's okay," Beau said. "I understand her concern. She's right to be cautious." He scratched the long, stubbled line of his jaw as he thought. "It's simple, really. I just want one thing in return for the money."

"What, our first born?" Johnny joked. "Free Macallan for life? Name it."

"Lola." Beau looked from Johnny to Lola with such intensity in his green eyes that she reached back to steady herself against a barstool. "I want Lola for one night."

Chapter Three

As if Beau's words had stopped time, Lola, Johnny and Beau stood frozen where they were. Lola didn't breathe. She might've thought Beau's proposition was a joke and even laughed if it weren't for his composure when he'd said it. As if to him, the deal were already made. He wanted Lola for one night, and that's what he'd have.

"Excuse me?" Lola asked so quietly, she wasn't entirely sure she'd spoken aloud.

Johnny stepped closer to the bar that separated him from Lola and Beau. He leaned his knuckles on the surface. "What the fuck did you just say?"

"Give me one night alone with Lola, and Hey Joe is yours."

"You're offering me money to sleep with my girlfriend?"

Lola hadn't blinked in so long, her eyes watered. When she did, her mind caught up. It raced ahead. Emotions came as fast as her heartbeat. *Thud.* Shock.

Thud. Indignation. *Thud.* Fear.

"What I'm offering you is your dream on a silver platter." Beau looked at Lola. "Both of you."

He had some nerve putting his eyes on her. Based on the last few hours, it wasn't even that surprising he'd come on to her. But to try to put a price on her—and on their time together? Her heartbeat was pure anger now, short, quick bursts that made her ears hot. "Fuck you," she said with her hands curled into two trembling balls. She wanted to say more, but she could only think of the crudest words possible. "Right, Johnny? Fuck him."

Johnny's neck reddened from his T-shirt to his jaw. Her concern shifted from herself to him. He looked like he might lunge for Beau, but Johnny wasn't a fighter. She'd never seen him lay an angry hand on anyone. She reached out to touch him, but he ripped his arm away and pounded his fist on the bar. "Tell me this is a sick joke, man," he said through a clenched jaw. That was Beau's cue to leave.

Beau raised one eyebrow. "I still don't have my answer."

"You want an answer?" Johnny asked. "How about I jump over this bar and give it to you with my fist?"

"I'm not looking for a fight," Beau said. "As long as we both have something the other wants, this can be worked out peacefully." He paused and removed his suit jacket by the lapels. "However," he said, tossing it over a stool, "we can do it your way too."

A door slammed in the back. Beau rolled up his shirtsleeves. She needed him gone before any of the staff came back out. She jerked her hand to the exit and said, "He told you to leave," but no sooner had she looked away from Johnny than he was ducking to get out from behind the bar.

Beau didn't move except to turn and face Johnny, who was already past Lola. Johnny seized Beau's crisp, white shirt. Beau's body stiffened as he drew up to his full height and met Johnny head on. Johnny drew his arm back. In that split second, instead of raising his own fist or trying to get loose, Beau looked at Lola. There was no fear in his expression, and that scared her more than anything. Johnny wasn't a fighter. She had no idea what Beau was capable of. Somebody would end up hurt, and it could very likely be the man she loved. She jumped up and latched onto Johnny's bicep.

"Stop!" Her feet were practically off the ground from giving Johnny's arm all her weight.

"Let go," Johnny said.

"Please don't do this, Johnny," she pleaded. "You won't win."

Johnny's head snapped toward her. The tension in his muscle immediately melted under her hands. "*What?*" he asked with his mouth hanging open.

Afraid Beau might sucker punch Johnny, she forced her way between them. More specifically, she pushed Johnny back behind her since Beau was immovable. "Get out," she told Beau.

Beau held her gaze while he picked up his jacket from the stool. He blinked over her head. "Five hundred thousand," he said to Johnny. "There's a number for you. That's what this place is worth give or take."

"What about what I'm worth?" Lola asked immediately.

Beau's eyes returned to hers.

Johnny grasped Lola's shoulders. "Move and let me handle this."

But Lola could not be moved as she locked eyes with Beau. In her hasty reply, she'd missed the number. Half a million dollars. It made her flush to be associated with any dollar amount, but this dollar amount was so high that she was absurdly impressed with herself. No person would walk into a bar and offer that to just anyone. It had to be something about *her*.

Lola tried to keep her thoughts from her face, but Beau looked as if he knew everything. She forced herself to see past the amount. It didn't matter whether this was about her specifically, because introducing money turned her from a person to a product. A service. The suggestion that she could be bought was a betrayal of her short but powerful time with Beau.

Beau raised his chin just noticeably. "What you're worth depends on whom you ask," he said to her. "If you want to know what you're worth to him, ask him his counteroffer. If you want to know what you're worth to me, bring me that counteroffer." He reached into his breast pocket and placed his card on the bar. "In case you change your minds," he said before walking away.

"We won't," she said.

He paused a moment then turned around. "Earlier, before we were interrupted, you asked me my opinion. I was going to say that you're captivating. You've held my attention from the start."

It wasn't until the door closed behind Beau that Lola lost the strength that'd been holding her together. Her legs trembled as she turned around to face Johnny. She put her face into his T-shirt. It smelled like him. She would never not know his scent. When she didn't feel his arms around her, she looked up into his face. His expressions were more familiar to her than her own, but this was one she didn't recognize.

"How could you say that?" he asked through his teeth.

She blinked at him a few times and took a step back. "What did I say?"

"'You won't win'? I was a second from pummeling him. Thanks for the vote of fucking confidence."

"Johnny, seriously? A fistfight? You're above that."

"Were we just in the same room?" he asked incredulously. "Did you not hear what he said?"

"Of course I heard. But it's not worth it. You're of more use to me here than in a jail cell. Or worse—a hospital bed."

"That's not why you stopped me," he said. "You didn't think I could take him."

Lola raked her fingers through her hair. She had too much on her mind to be stroking Johnny's ego. "Everything happened so fast. If you'd seen the look in his eyes—"

"I did. I was standing right in front of him."

She shook her head quickly. "You didn't see what I saw. I said that to protect you. One or both of you could've gotten really hurt. You don't know his background. He could be dangerous."

"Don't ever get in the middle like that again," he said. "You could've been the one hurt. I don't need *you* to protect *me*."

Vero came out from the backroom, whistling with her bag swinging over her arm. "You guys ready to lock up? The others went out the back, and I got somewhere to be."

"Yeah, let's get the fuck out of here," Johnny muttered, walking to the front to shut out the lights.

"What'd the suit want?" Vero asked. "He going to make an offer?"

"No," Lola snapped, already headed the opposite direction to get her purse from the back. When she returned, the bar was dark and empty. She heard Johnny start the car. On her way out, she remembered Beau's card on the counter. She went back to throw it away—it was the last thing she wanted to see when they came in the next day.

It was gone.

◆ ◆ ◆

Lola rubbed her wrist where her watch had been. Johnny brushed his teeth so hard, she heard the whole thing from where she sat on the edge of their bed.

It was always the normal-looking guys who were deranged. Given her past, she could usually spot them, but this guy, Beau—who seemed to be things she wasn't used to, like charming and refined—that level of depravity on a guy like him surprised her.

The ride home had been quiet. She'd gone over her brief conversations with Beau for any clue of what was to come. The only thing out of the ordinary was his sudden coldness toward her at the end when she wouldn't accept his tip.

She'd apologized to Johnny right before they'd gotten out of the car, but he'd sullenly ignored her. Her mind had still been playing catch up. Something in particular had nagged at her—she just couldn't figure out what.

The faucet stopped and Johnny came out of the ensuite bathroom in his boxers. He leaned in the doorway with his arms crossed. "What interrupted you?"

"What?" Lola asked.

He sighed irritably as if she'd checked out of a conversation she hadn't known they were having. "He said you guys were interrupted before he could say you were 'captivating.' What interrupted you?"

"It was early in the night," she said, swallowing. "I don't really remember."

"Try," he said.

Lola glanced at her hands. Beau had been standing across from her with his loosened tie and easy grin. Earlier. Before he'd become visibly stiff in those last moments. What had he said to her? That it was hard to get his attention, but that she had it. Such bold disregard for her relationship excited her more than it should. Nobody she knew went after anything that way—except maybe her before she'd settled down with Johnny. "I think he was trying to…to flirt with me, I guess, but you came out from the back," Lola said. "That's when I introduced you. He was being a little forward."

"Why didn't you tell me? I would've thrown him out."

"Because I can handle myself," she said. "Besides, you told me to flirt with him at the end of the night."

"Not *really* flirt," Johnny said tersely. "I meant in a way that he thinks you're flirting but you're really not. Whatever." He pushed off the doorjamb. "So did you give him a reason to make that offer?"

"Johnny," she scolded. "It's *me*. The woman you love and who loves you back." She waited, hoping his expression would clear a little. "Of course I didn't give him a reason. The whole thing was stupid."

"Come here," he said.

"What?"

"I said come over here."

She stood slowly and went to him. He took her chin and kissed her. Her upper lip pinched between their teeth, and she jerked back. "Johnny, stop. We need to talk about this."

"Later," he said. With a hand on her shoulder, he gently nudged her toward the bed.

"It's four in the morning."

"Yeah." He pulled her against him by her hips and kissed her again. He ran his hand down her backside and squeezed. "Right now, you know what I want."

She knew. Most of the time when they had sex, it was after she and Johnny had fallen into bed, or in the late morning when they woke up. Once in a while, though, Johnny got really worked up, and then he liked her on her hands and knees.

She turned around willingly. When Johnny had his rare urges, he didn't fight them, and she didn't want him to. Those were the times he went absolutely crazy for her.

She climbed onto the bed in only a long T-shirt. He lifted it up and grabbed her ass in both hands. He rubbed against her. She dropped her forehead toward the mattress as he entered her. His first few thrusts were long and slow as she warmed up to him, but they soon turned quick and hard. It normally took time for her to climax from penetration alone, but she almost always did this way. She became putty in his hands to know he was so consumed, he couldn't even bother with foreplay.

"That's it. Damn, Lo," Johnny said. "You feel good."

She gasped. "Right there. Don't stop."

"You like that?" He ran a hand up her back, then grabbed her hips and pulled her into his next thrust. "Like it hard, baby? How's that for fucking flirting?"

Her breath caught. He was thinking of Beau, which made her think of Beau. "What?"

Johnny pulled out and slid himself up between her cheeks.

"Johnny—"

"Please, babe. Just for a minute. I need this."

"No," she said. She had no interest in anal, especially when Johnny was like this.

He breathed out some complaint she didn't catch

and was inside her again as if he'd never left.

Beau had been planted in her mind, though—his flirtatious, lopsided smile.

His sexy red tie, sexy five o'clock shadow, *sexy, sexy, sexy*—and she was so sure he had a nice, big cock to back up that suggestive grin.

Oh, God. Yes.

Maybe he'd even wear his suit while fucking her from behind, too eager to bother undressing.

Yes! Just like that.

He'd pull her hair and tell her how badly he'd wanted her from the moment he'd laid eyes on her.

Lola toppled into a viscous climax as Beau's image seared into her memory. Almost as quickly, guilt flooded in. Johnny didn't last much longer.

After he'd come, he smoothed a hand over her backside and up her back. He squeezed her shoulder. "You good?"

"Yes," she said. She was breathless, not from her orgasm, but because she'd never thought about another man while she was with Johnny. Ever.

When he pulled out, she practically ran to bathroom. She locked the door behind her, turned and confronted herself in the mirror. It was a serious crime, yes. But it wasn't even her fault. Johnny had brought Beau into bed with them. There were worse things. She was only human. In the desperate moments before an orgasm, there were no rules. It was what she'd needed to cross the finish line—the thought of Beau inside her. Her sensitive clit was already throbbing again.

She forced herself to calm down so she could

return to the bedroom. Johnny sat with his back against the headboard and his long legs extended in front of him. He knew. The look on his face said everything. He had to know she'd been thinking of Beau in their most intimate moment.

"So if he was flirtatious with you before I met him, that means he had his eye on you from the beginning," Johnny said. "Right?"

Lola hid her relief that he didn't suspect she'd been fantasizing. She took a tentative step toward the bed. This was a conversation best had once they'd slept on things, but Johnny didn't look like he wanted to wait. "I guess," Lola said. "Unless he was just there looking for anyone."

"What about your dart game? Did he say anything then?"

She rolled her lips together and shook her head.

"Because he made a weird comment during pool that I ignored, but now it makes more sense."

"What comment?" Lola asked, edging closer and sitting at his feet.

"He asked if I kept Amanda around to make myself feel good. Right in front of her."

Lola caught her laugh before it escaped. It reminded her of something Veronica would say if Lola'd ever let her. It became less funny, though, when she wondered what would make an outsider like Beau even ask that. "Amanda does flirt with you," Lola said.

Johnny shrugged. "It's Amanda. She's just like that. You've said it doesn't bother you enough to get rid of her."

"It doesn't, because I know you. I know us. Give me the same credit, and don't hold me to a double standard about the flirting."

He waved a dismissive hand. "Amanda's harmless. I wouldn't even notice if she stopped showing up for work, except that we'd be one person short."

"So Beau made a couple harmless comments too. I can handle myself. You were nearby if I needed you."

"You're comparing *him* to Amanda?"

Lola sighed. "Just to show that it was no big deal until it was. So what'd you say when Beau asked you that?"

"I said no, I keep her around because she's a good waitress. Then he looked at you and said I already had the best waitress around, so why the fuck would I need anyone else? He actually said *fuck*, like he was pissed or something. Amanda sulked, then it was my turn to shoot and that was the end of it."

"I don't get it," Lola said, shaking her head. "Nobody in their right mind would pay that much for one night of anything, even sex. Do you think he was being serious?"

Johnny sat forward on the bed. "He wanted to get laid. He's got money to burn. Must've figured we were hard up for cash and low on decency."

No matter how Lola looked at it, it didn't add up. A man like that wouldn't have any problem getting women. Even if he did, there were not-so-secret secret call girl services for men with his kind of money. She'd known a girl or two who'd been through that. "Maybe he has a very specific taste," Lola murmured.

"For what?"

"I don't know. Maybe I'm his type."

Johnny had calmed down. She could sense it with him, but it never took him long to return to his easygoing self. He held out his hand and beckoned her. She moved to sit on her knees next to him.

"You know I think you're the most beautiful girl in five states. I see the way guys look at you when you're waiting tables. Great figure, nice tits."

"*Nice?*"

"Incredible, babe."

"What're you getting at?" she asked.

"Nothing. I just don't think that's enough to pay for one night what I don't even make in a decade."

Lola finally pinpointed what'd been bothering her on the ride home—Beau's insinuation that Johnny could put a dollar amount on Lola. He'd suggested a counteroffer as if one existed and they just hadn't found it yet. "How much would you say I'm worth then?" Lola asked.

Johnny took her arm and pulled her forward. She leaned in for a more intimate moment than they'd had all night. "Don't take it that way," he said, kissing her once on the lips. "I respect you too much to even answer that." He kissed her again and lay back on the bed, getting under the covers.

"It's a lot of money," she said quietly.

He fluffed his pillow. "I know you're worried about Hey Joe, but it'll all work out. I bet you Mitch gets cold feet and ends up not selling."

Lola stayed where she was, staring at the wall by

the bed. He sounded so confident, but she didn't share his optimism. During the last few conversations she'd had with the owner about Hey Joe, stress had etched his face. "Johnny, did you ever think about buying the bar?"

"Guess so, here and there. Kind of feels like mine already. But never seriously or anything."

"That's the best of both worlds," Lola said. "You get the bar you love, and you don't have to start from the ground up."

"It'd be like owning a piece of history," Johnny agreed. "Rock 'n' roll history. We could get it back to what it was, you and me."

Lola glanced down at him. "What's the first thing you'd do?"

"I'd work my ass off to get good music in there again. Maybe serve some food. Open earlier in the day. People in the door, no matter what it took."

She smiled at him. She liked the times where Johnny got caught up in something bigger than their life. "You could run that place with your eyes closed."

"With you by my side, sure could." They grinned at each other, sharing the same dream. It faded from Johnny's eyes. "What're you saying, Lo?"

"I don't know. Mitch hasn't bothered with the day to day for so long that, like you said, sometimes the bar feels like ours. But I never imagined actually owning it until tonight. I didn't think it was a possibility for us."

"And what, it is now?" he asked.

"No," she said emphatically. She got under the covers too and snuggled against his side. "I told you my dad loved bikes. He used to collect Harley gear for the day he'd own one. I promised I'd buy him one when I got older. That was before he left, obviously. Sad thing is, even if I could buy him one, I wouldn't know where to find him." She paused, tracing one of the tattoos on Johnny's chest. "I've never made someone's dream come true. Or given them anything."

"You made my dream come true."

She looked up at him. "I did?"

"I have you, don't I? That's something money can't buy." He smiled and smoothed his hand over her hairline. "Don't worry, babe. We'll figure something out."

"But by then, Hey Joe might not be around anymore," Lola said. They'd been figuring things out since they'd started dating. Lola still thought about going back to school *some day*. *Some day*, Johnny would propose. They'd talked about having kids *some day* when they'd saved more and could afford things like a bigger apartment.

Starting a business didn't fit into any of that. It occurred to her that though Johnny wanted those things, he wouldn't go after them. He would wait for them to happen to him or for Lola to tell him it was time. Her role was to move them forward, a reality she'd conveniently ignored—until Beau had opened her eyes to it. If neither of them did anything, they'd be in this bed ten years from now, wondering why they didn't have the things they'd always hoped for.

Lola switched off the bedside lamp, turned back and kissed his chest. "It's stupid, but right after my dad left, I thought if I could just get him that bike, he'd come back. Like me plus a bike would be enough for him." She looked up at him. "Is this enough for you? If we never got further than where we are right now?"

He was quiet.

"Johnny?" she asked.

No answer. He'd fallen asleep.

Chapter Four

Lola heaped potato salad onto Mark's plate. He looked at it, then back up. "That it?"

"You know the rule. Nobody gets seconds until everyone's had a helping."

"Six growing men at this picnic table, Lola."

She rolled her eyes. "If any of you are still growing, it's sideways, not up."

He pulled on his belt with his free hand and grinned. "Come on, Mama. Give your second favorite man a little extra love."

"You want more potato salad, walk your ass over to Pavilions and get it yourself. Next!"

Mark muttered as he went around Lola to sit down.

Johnny and his friends played football in the park some weekends while Lola and a few other wives and girlfriends set up food for afterward. It was a good spot, even for busy afternoons, with a playground nearby for the kids.

Johnny stood quietly with his plate between them as Lola served him.

"Everything all right?" she asked. Their morning had been normal despite their unusual night. Neither of them had brought up Beau or his offer. Johnny had even been in high spirits for football. During the game, though, Lola had looked over at a commotion and seen Johnny arguing with Mark before spiking the football hard into the grass.

"I'm fine."

"You mad because your side lost?" He wasn't a sore loser, but it was the only plausible reason for his shift in mood.

"I said I'm fine."

"Okay." She smiled and scooped him more potato salad. "A little extra for my man," she said. "Don't tell Mark."

"Thanks, babe," he said and pressed a quick kiss to the top of her head.

Lola sat across from Johnny once she'd made herself a plate. Mark gestured as he told everyone about the harrowing adventure of taking his six-year-old son to the mall. They'd gone to find his wife a birthday present, only to go home empty-handed because his credit card had been declined.

"Maybe that's because you're at a picnic in the middle of a workday," Johnny said.

"Shop's closed for renovations this weekend, asshole. You calling me out in front of my wife?"

"Now, now, boys." Brenda smiled. "Mark and Kyle ended up surprising me by setting up the Slip 'N Slide in the backyard. We played in the sprinklers all day. Couldn't have asked for a better birthday."

Mark put his arm around Brenda's shoulders.

Johnny winked at Lola. He held up a forkful of potato salad before cleaning it off in one bite.

Mark's son ran from the playground to the table. He stuck his shoe on the bench. "Tie," he demanded.

"Kyle, why don't you show everyone how you've been learning to tie your own shoes?"

"I don't want to," Kyle said.

"I'll do it, buddy," Lola said. Kyle ran over to her. She snuck him a smile as she fixed his shoe. "You know how to do this, don't you?"

"Yeah."

"So I'll tie this one, and you can show me how you do it on your left shoe."

"But that one's not untied," he said.

Lola reached down and yanked one of the laces. "There you go."

"Lola," he cried out, raising his arms in the same exasperated way his dad often did.

"Come on," she said. "Your daddy's been bragging about this all week. But I never believe anything until I see it with my own eyes."

Kyle made a face but swapped feet on the bench and went to work. "I got it," he said, brushing her hands away when she went to help. After a few tries, he hollered "I did it" and took off back to the other kids.

"You're good with him," Brenda said to her.

"When you grow up without brothers or sisters, everything kids do is entertaining," Lola said.

"Well, you're welcome to take him any time and see all the entertaining things he does." Mark laughed. "Love that little shit, but can't say I'm not glad school starts next week."

Brenda turned to Johnny. "Wasn't she good with Kyle?"

Johnny half rolled his eyes.

"Aw, come on," she said. "Indulge me."

"Our answer's still the same," he said. "Kids cost money. Right, babe?"

She almost said they were figuring it out. The night before might not have come up again, but Lola hadn't forgotten anything. Her eyes were now widely open to their inaction. As long as they were 'figuring it out,' she and Johnny weren't doing much of anything. Her chest was tight.

"There's never a good time," Brenda said. "Mark and I were still living at my mom's when I got knocked up. You just have to go for it."

"Maybe Lola's waiting for Johnny to propose sometime this century," Mark said.

"With what, a fucking cucumber?" Johnny asked, visibly irritated.

"Why not?" Lola asked. "I don't need anything fancy."

Johnny's fork stopped halfway to his mouth as his eyes cut to her.

"We could do it here in the park," she said, sitting up a little straighter. "Maybe Mitch would donate some beer to cut down on costs. It could be a small thing, friends and family only."

Brenda clasped her hands together. "That's a great idea," she exclaimed. "We'll find you a vintage dress for next to nothing on Melrose."

Lola wasn't the type to get swept away. She'd never thought much about her wedding day like the girls she knew, but the idea of something simple brought a smile to her face. "That sounds nice, doesn't it, Johnny?"

"Sure," he said as he forked a watermelon chunk. "Tell you what. We'll pick up a lottery ticket on the way home and if I win, that cucumber'll have a big, fat diamond on it."

Someone laughed uncomfortably.

Johnny chewed, looking around the table. "What? It was a joke. Except maybe the lottery ticket. Now *that* is a good idea."

Lola blinked at him. "The lottery?"

"Since when do you play the lottery?" Mark asked.

"Since today. Might as well. Not like my life is going anywhere." Johnny squinted into the distance, just beyond Lola. "Brenda, be a doll and pass a lemon square over here."

The table got even quieter, but Lola barely noticed. She didn't care about a wedding, but she didn't like the way he'd just dismissed her and their life together.

She ignored Johnny the rest of the meal, which wasn't hard since he kept to himself. After, she cleared off the picnic table alone so the other women could get their kids ready to go.

"Need help with that?" Johnny asked from a few feet away.

She glanced up at him. "What was that just now?

Were you trying to embarrass me?"

"No, just myself." He stuck his hands in his back pockets. "Mission accomplished," he joked.

She tossed paper plates into a large garbage bag. "I don't care about a wedding. I thought the park was a nice idea, but that's all. I don't need it."

"I know you don't need it. You never need anything or anyone. But you deserve more than this crap." He gestured at the dirty table. "I want you to have a nice ring and a Hawaiian wedding."

"*Hawaii?*" She rested the bag on the bench. "What are you talking about?"

"When we were younger, you said you wanted to go to Hawaii one day because it sounded romantic. Remember?"

"No," Lola said. "I never think about Hawaii. We could get married at the Pomona Swap Meet for all I care." She tossed some plastic silverware and resumed cleaning. "We don't have to get married at all, Johnny. We've been fine without it this long. But I'll tell you one thing—we're not doing it in Hawaii."

"Why not?" he asked.

"Why would you even want to?"

"Last night got me thinking about how we never splurge," Johnny said. "You were right yesterday when you said time off would be good for us."

Lola shook her head, grabbed a beer bottle and poured the remains onto the grass. "I think you should forget about last night."

After a beat, he asked, "Have you?"

She dropped the bottle in the bag and picked up

another. She didn't like lying to Johnny and hadn't forgotten about last night. "No, but I'm trying."

"Yeah, well. I don't blame you. I'd feel pretty special if someone thought my dick was worth half a mil."

He clearly had a bone to pick with her. Lola wanted to get to the root of what bothered him, but not when he acted like that. She picked up the garbage bag. On her way past him, she said, "I don't know what your problem is, but you're being a real jerk." She walked briskly to the nearest trashcan and dumped the bag in it. When she turned around, he was behind her.

"You're right," he said. "It was a lame attempt to be funny. I'm sorry."

She crossed her arms. "Are you going to tell me what's wrong? Otherwise I need you to take me home so I can get the laundry done before work tonight."

He looked at his feet and slowly rubbed his hands together. "The thing is, part of me hoped that whole thing last night was a joke. It wasn't. I looked Beau up this morning while you were in the shower."

Lola pursed her lips. She wasn't angry because he'd done it, but because all day, during any moment she'd had alone, she'd been fighting herself not to do the same thing. "And?"

"He could probably buy Hawaii if he wanted. He really does have that kind of money, and apparently he's got lots of women to choose from." Their eyes met, and Johnny frowned. "It's intimidating that a guy like that wants my girlfriend."

Lola's shoulders loosened. The moment either of

them started to feel insecure about their relationship was the moment they opened it up to problems. "You're looking at it wrong," she said sympathetically. "You have something he wants but can't have. In fact, maybe the *only* thing a guy like that can't have. That should make you feel good."

"Except that it doesn't. He's a millionaire. I've been working since I was seventeen with nothing to show for it. I'm an asshole. And I suck at football."

One corner of Lola's mouth rose. "You're the best one out there."

"You have to say that because you're my girlfriend."

"True, but it doesn't mean shit. Those guys are terrible."

He chuckled. "Yeah. We're pretty bad."

"You should all stick to video games."

He pretended to look hurt. "Geez, you don't have to drill the point home."

She uncrossed her arms. "And you aren't an asshole. I bet in order to get to that level of success, Beau had to step on some people. You'd never do that. You're a good person, Johnny. That's what matters in the end."

He considered that a moment. Lola saw their friends heading for their cars. Thinking the conversation was over, she started to walk away, but Johnny said, "He's a venture capitalist."

Lola paused. "What?"

"Beau. He invests in tech startups, but before that, he built a website that sold for millions."

"Oh." Lola wasn't impressed. She was more concerned with why Johnny was still talking about it.

"According to the article I read online," Johnny continued, "it took him like a decade to do it. He would build a website, but either someone else would beat him to it or he couldn't get investors. He didn't give up, though, even when the market crashed. Took him seven times before something finally stuck."

Lola's throat was dry. That only reiterated one of the few things she knew for sure about Beau Olivier. "He's persistent," she said.

"The company that bought his website ended up squashing it or something, so it never saw the light of day. Now he's co-founder of Bolt Ventures." Johnny shrugged. "Did all that, and he never even went to college."

Lola knew that already, but she didn't see the point in mentioning it. Despite her curiosity about Beau's background, the less she knew the better. She changed the subject. "Johnny, unless you're planning on going commando tomorrow, I need to do laundry today."

He furrowed his eyebrows. "I could've sworn I just did it."

"That was *two* months ago," she cried with a burst of laughter. "Where do you think your clean clothes come from, invisible fairies?"

Johnny grinned and waved her off. "Hey," he said. "Come here."

She took a few steps, put a hand on her cocked hip and narrowed her eyes playfully. "What?"

"I'll take you to Hawaii one day. Or wherever you

want to go. Even if it's the goddamn Pomona Swap Meet. I promise."

Lola dropped her arm from her hip and sighed. He'd flinched when he'd said *Hawaii*. She didn't know how to make it any clearer to him that Hawaii meant nothing to her. But as she was on the verge of starting up the argument again, she stopped herself. His eyes weren't as hard as they had been the last few hours, and she didn't want to provoke him. The back and forth was beginning to drain her.

Instead, she said, "I appreciate that, but I don't need to go anywhere. I'm fine as long as I have one thing."

He spoke before she could say *you*. "Clean underwear?" he guessed.

She rolled her eyes and smiled. "Yes. As long as I have that."

◆ ◆ ◆

Later, at the Laundromat down the street, Lola unloaded clothing from her basket into a washer. All three of the functioning machines at her complex had been occupied, which was why she normally avoided doing laundry on the weekends. She straightened up and rubbed her lower back. She'd never owned her own washer and dryer, but that was certainly something she'd be willing to splurge on with her five hundred grand. She covered her mouth at the thought and checked to make sure no one was around, as if she'd said it aloud.

She grabbed Johnny's jeans and emptied change

from the pockets into a baggie like always. Lint and a movie stub went in the trash. The last thing she pulled out was a white business card with corners rigid enough to break skin. There was a phone number and a company name. She flipped it over. It was as vague and mysterious as the man it belonged to. Across the front was only his name, printed in stiff, sharp letters.

Beau Olivier.

Chapter Five

Vero whistled low, craning her neck to see through the neon maze that was Hey Joe's front window. "Check out those wheels."

The door was propped open for the seventy-degree weather. In the early-evening dusk, a man in a suit got out of an Audi. Lola and Johnny, crowded behind the bar with Vero, looked at each other.

"Let me handle this," he said.

"What's going on?" Vero asked. "Is it the money guy?"

Lola's gaze snapped between Veronica and Johnny. "You told her?"

"Personally, I would've accepted the offer," Vero said, a teasing smile on her face. "Wonder how he feels about redheads."

"It's prostitution," Lola said.

"I prefer to think of it as a trade." Vero opened her hand toward the door. "You got something I want," she pointed at her crotch, "I got something you want."

"So you sleep with him then," Lola said.

"Honey, for that much I would. I don't care how he looks." She leaned over so Johnny couldn't hear. "But damn if that man didn't look *good.*"

Lola shook her head. "He looked like trouble."

Vero laughed throatily. "You know Vero gives it up to trouble for free all the time."

Lola willed herself to look away from the door. It'd been days since Beau had been there. She hated to admit she was still thinking of him. There had to have been a reason he picked her, but she went in circles trying to figure it out. Had there been others? If so, what was the common factor between them?

She tore her eyes away to focus on Johnny. He watched the door with more intensity than he'd looked at her with in days. A few hours earlier, an unusually large table of male customers had ordered round after round. He'd joked with them that if they doubled their bill by the end of the night, he'd throw in a complimentary lap dance from the waitress of their choice. "Come on, I'm joking around" had been his defensive answer to her glare. Johnny didn't joke around like that, but he hadn't really been himself since the picnic.

Lola held her breath when the man walked in. She and Johnny exhaled at the same time. "It's not him," Johnny said in a way that almost sounded disappointed. Johnny leaned over the bar. "Can I help you?"

In the light, the man was clearly not Beau. His arms were too short for his wrinkled suit jacket and his belly strained the buttons of his dress shirt. "Wow," he said. He narrowed his eyes up and around, stopping at the framed black-and-white photos of musicians on Hey Joe's stage. "This is even more authentic than it looked on the Internet. Not like the dives you see in Brooklyn where all the stuff on the walls came from a website or boutique."

Vero was refilling the bar caddies. Johnny picked up a jar of olives she'd asked him to open earlier and knocked the lid hard against the edge of the bar. Everyone jumped and turned to him. He twisted off the top and passed it to Vero without removing his eyes from the man. "What can I do for you?"

He held out his hand for Johnny, who just stared at it. "Hank Walken," he said, jovial and unaffected by the brushoff.

"Jonathan Pace."

"I'm looking for Mr. Wegley."

"Mitch isn't around right now. What's this about?"

"Heard this place is for sale. You guys worked here long?"

"About twelve years," Johnny said.

"How's business?"

The man was smarmy. Lola would set the building on fire before a guy like that got his hands on Hey Joe. "It sucks," Lola said. "In fact, the whole block sucks."

Hank nodded. "Interesting."

"Interesting?" Johnny asked.

Hank scanned the wall behind them. "Yeah," he said absentmindedly. "It's got a lot of potential. Would do well with some sprucing up."

Johnny and Lola exchanged a look. "Sprucing up how?"

"I've done my homework. This place has history. Foot traffic. Repeat business." Hank checked under the lip of the bar as if he expected to find something there. "That's not showing in the numbers, though. It needs a fresh touch. Something special. Maybe a rooftop bar or a lounge area or something."

"This is more of a local joint," Johnny said.

Hank's eyes went to a pool game happening in the corner. "I picked up on that."

"It's the complete opposite of a lounge."

"There's your problem." Hank pointed at Johnny, grinning. "You're not thinking outside the box, son. It's all about the angle. We give it a cool, hip, rock 'n' roll vibe. Get some young celebrities to make appearances at the reopening. We've already got the rep, but a new look and a little rebranding could do wonders." He nodded thoughtfully to no one in particular. "I've flipped bars before, and fives minutes in here, I'm seeing a lot of missed opportunities."

It was exactly what Lola and Johnny had been saying for years. Mitch wasn't willing to budge on a lot of things to keep the integrity of the bar, but sales suffered as a result. Not that Lola and Johnny had ever once discussed turning it into a lounge. "What opportunities?" Lola asked.

Hank looked back at her and narrowed his eyes. "Think I got this far by giving away my secrets, sweetheart?" He laughed good-naturedly but didn't answer her question.

"Business really is slow," she said. "Not sure this place can be saved."

"I disagree," Hank said. "In the right hands, Hey Joe could be at least doubling profits by this time next year." He dug his sausage-like fingers into his suit jacket. "I'll give you my card. I'm just going to take a look around. If I don't hear from Mr. Wegley, I'll try again tomorrow."

Johnny took the card. "He won't be in until Friday."

"Any way we can get him in here to take a meeting?"

"He's out of town."

"Guess I should've called before hopping on a flight from New York. That's all right. I'll wait."

Hank walked away. He swiveled his head, pausing to read Lola's flyers on a corkboard. He inspected the floors, touched the walls—got so close to the pool table, a man nearly twice his size asked him if he knew any surgeons who specialized in pool-cue removal.

Johnny held up the card for Lola, ripped it and dropped it in the trash behind the bar. "Are you kidding me? A rooftop bar?"

Lola shook her head. "Can you imagine if Quartz and the guys heard that?"

"Hey Joe's got history, man," Johnny said. His eyes narrowed on Hank as he made his slow way to the exit. "Seriously. You can't just flush that down the toilet."

Vero shrugged. "Something needs to change. Maybe it's time, Boss."

"And maybe you go snort some lines," he said.

"Johnny," Lola scolded. "What is with you?"

He muttered an apology, grabbed a Coors from the mini-fridge and keyed off the top. Vero muttered about checking on her tables. Lola kept her mouth shut and didn't mention Johnny's no-drinking-during-work-hours rule.

Vero hadn't put anything away. Lola picked up the jar of olives, but it slipped out of her hands and broke. "Damn it," she cried, jumping back. "Why don't you guys ever clean up your own shit?"

"You guys?" Johnny asked.

Lola glanced up at him. She saw an opening for her frustration and took it. "Yes, *you guys*. Did you not see the basket of clean laundry that's been sitting out since Saturday?"

Johnny's lips pinched. "I thought you were waiting to put it away."

"Waiting for what?" Lola asked. "There's no law that says you can't do it."

He held up a palm and the beer in his hand. "Sorry. I didn't realize it was a test."

"It wasn't," Lola said under her breath, squatting to clean up the glass. "It would just be nice if someone else did something once in a while." She'd overreacted. It was second nature to clean up after Johnny and that transferred over to work. But the constantly taking things out and leaving them there annoyed her sometimes.

She dropped the big pieces of glass in the trash, right on top of the two halves of Hank's card. "Johnny?"

"What?" he asked. "I said I was sorry."

"No, not that." She paused. "Where's Beau's card?"

Johnny stopped staring into space and turned abruptly to her. "Why?"

"I remember him setting it on the bar, but I never threw it out. Just wondering what happened to it…"

Johnny took a long swig of his drink. He inspected the bottle. "I tossed it."

"That night?"

"Yeah."

"When?"

"Like I said, that fucking night, right after he left. Ripped it in half too. Should I have burned it?"

Lola looked at him as hard as he avoided looking at her. After finding Beau's card in Johnny's pocket, she'd hidden it in her birth control box under the sink—and it was in one piece. "Are you sure?"

"Yeah, I'm goddamn sure, Lola," he said. "What're you nagging me for?"

Vero walked up and set a ticket on the bar. Johnny snatched it to fill the order. Lola tried to convince herself she owed her boyfriend the benefit of the doubt, but that he'd kept the card meant only one thing to her. However small it was, there was a part of Johnny considering Beau's offer.

◆ ◆ ◆

Mitch returned to work that Friday. It'd been a long, draining week of mood swings and clipped words—

offenses both Lola and Johnny were guilty of.

While Johnny was distracted up front, Lola went back to Mitch's office and leaned in the doorway.

"What is it?" he asked without removing his eyes from his computer.

"How was your trip?"

"Productive. Barb found a house she likes."

"I bet her family is happy you guys are moving there."

"They are." Mitch looked up. "Barb is too. She's wanted this for some time."

"What about you?" Lola asked.

"You know how it is. This place is a grind. Barb always said if it got to be too much, she wanted me out."

"But do you have to leave L.A.?"

He held his arms out. "This *is* L.A. Things were great when I was out there screwing around with customers all day, but now I'm back here most of the time, trying to dig myself out of this hole. Barb knows my dad's place is the only thing keeping me in California."

"Yeah." Lola picked at some peeling paint. "Have you had any offers?"

"Nothing official yet, but it won't be long."

"Oh."

"What is it, Lola? I'm kind of busy here."

"I don't know. I just…Mitch, what do you think this place needs? Why's business slow?"

He sighed. "In the eighties, when my dad handed over the reins, we were already struggling. But then grunge came on the scene and I wasn't letting that anywhere near here. Not after the rock legends we'd seen."

"So you lost the young music crowd."

"Young and some old. You know all this, Lola."

"I'm trying to see it from a business perspective."

"All right, then you want to know my first mistake? Pay for play. I let my head get too big asking new bands to cough up cash for a spot on our stage. They walked instead. I could've made up for it in the nineties, but like I said, I fucking hate grunge. Turns out a lot of people don't, though. When Fred's went belly up, the block became a carousel of crap. Except us, the only place still standing, but our knees are buckling. Barb says I either sell out or get out, so I'm washing my hands of it. I can't stick around to see what happens."

Mitch's words were hard, but she heard the regret in his voice. "That Hank guy said something about a lounge. I think he wants to turn this place high end."

"We're meeting later today, so I'll know more then, but it sounds like he wants to keep the name and image, just make it into something classier. A real scene."

"But that's not what Hey Joe is." That wasn't what Johnny was.

He shrugged. "Not really, kid. Sorry."

"Would you say this place is a good investment?"

"There'll never not be foot traffic. Just about getting back on the map."

Lola felt her heartbeat everywhere. In the last week, she'd struggled more than ever with the pressure to take care of Johnny in a bigger way than she had been. Now it was more than that. Lola could bring herself to walk away from Hey Joe, but that didn't mean it wasn't worth saving for Johnny, for all the other people who loved it and for its history. She might be the only one who could do it. "So if someone had the opportunity to buy it, they should take it?"

"Whatever you're thinking, forget it. You don't know anybody with that kind of money."

"I might."

"I know Johnny's got his heart set on owning a bar and believe me, I'd love to make that happen for you two. Nobody knows this place like him. But there's no way in hell you can even ballpark the offers I'm hearing."

"What're the offers, Mitch?"

"Around six hundred grand," he said.

Lola looked at the floor. More than Beau's proposition—but people took out small business loans all the time, didn't they? Maybe not for that much, but the difference? She cleared her throat. "If Johnny and I could come up with the money—"

"Hey," Mitch said, shaking his head. "Come on. You and Johnny are good kids. You've always been straight. Don't tell me that's changed."

"Hypothetically."

Mitch bit the end of his pen and reclined in his seat, studying her. "If you can make me a decent offer, and if you're upfront with yourselves about the hard work ahead of you, then you should. Hypothetically? Buying this bar would be easier than Johnny starting his own, but not much considering the state of things. It's not like I want to see my dad's place destroyed, but I can't feed myself off my principles anymore. Once I get my check, it's out of my hands."

Lola returned to the front of the house. Johnny poured three shots in his bartender's rhythm, one at a time and without stopping. Lola stayed off to the side. He said something to the three girls in front of him as he patted his beer gut and laughed. That beer gut had been a valley nine years ago when she'd started dating a tall, skinny, twenty-four-year-old Johnny with darkish hair past his ears—hair that was now down to his shoulder blades and always in a ponytail. The valley was now a small hill. That beer gut had history. She liked it and what it stood for.

Johnny wouldn't survive a new owner. He'd been doing things his way for too long. And she sure as hell wouldn't stick around without him. Nobody liked change, especially not Johnny, and it was on the horizon, speeding their way.

◆ ◆ ◆

The ride home that night was quiet. Lola went over the numbers in her head again and again. If Walken bought Hey Joe, she figured they could be out of their jobs within weeks. She listed alternatives. They'd both have to hustle, because even though Lola had been thinking lately she might like to try something new, they couldn't survive on Johnny's wages alone. She'd have to work while she figured her shit out. Fall classes had already started, so school was out of the question for a few months at least.

She looked over at Johnny as he pulled into their apartment complex. He'd been preoccupied, but not about losing their jobs. It was as if he expected everything to just figure itself out—the way he expected getting married, having kids and owning a business would happen on their own. He was thirty-three. They'd been driving through a tunnel for the last eight years, and they were about to come out of the darkness. She couldn't see what was on the other side, but at least *she* was trying.

"Johnny?" she asked when they'd parked and he reached for the handle.

He looked back. "Yeah?"

"You're my best friend."

"It's late, babe."

She smiled, a little resigned. "I know. But you are. When we're young, we think we're invincible. Then we get older, and it's like we realize not everything works out all the time. If you want certain things, you have to put in the effort for them. Or even make sacrifices."

Johnny put his hand over hers on the seat. "What's bringing this on?"

She squinted out the windshield. "Money was a big deal to my mom. She would say 'The toaster's broken. We got no money, so we have to live with broken toasters and ripped screen doors that won't even keep out a fly, forget about a robber.' I had no idea who'd want to rob us. We had nothing. She said that was naïve and stupid, because desperate people were everywhere.

"She told me money was the reason my dad left.

There wasn't enough. So I believed money and happiness were inextricably linked until I met you and decided love was more important. I was in a dark place, but you came in and saved me. Since then, I've tried hard to convince myself money isn't important at all."

Johnny sniffed. "Now you realize it is."

"Mitch said something to me today. He said, 'I can't feed myself off my principles anymore.' It's kind of the same with love. Those things are so much, Johnny, but they aren't everything like I wish they were. Money can give us stability and freedom. It can give us choices."

Johnny released her hand and ran his palms down his pants to his knees. "Life is easier with working appliances," he said flatly.

"If someone buys the bar, we'll probably lose our jobs."

"I know."

"Do you know? You're more concerned about Hey Joe being glamorized than you are about how we'll survive."

"I don't see the point in worrying about it until we know more," he said. "Something could still happen."

"Something like what?" Lola asked. If Johnny said it out loud, she wouldn't have to. Not knowing if he wanted her to accept the offer was almost worse than if he'd just come out and tell her to do it. She was stuck, and she had no idea which door would lead to their happiness.

"I don't know," he admitted. "But there's still time."

"There isn't any more time," Lola said. "Are we stupid not to take the only exit we'll ever get? Buying the bar isn't just keeping our jobs. It's following your dream. It's building a life and having a steady income and saving a legacy. All in one night."

"So what're you saying?" Johnny asked. He wouldn't look at her. "You want my permission to sleep with another man?"

Lola turned in her seat to face him. "I don't look at it that way," she said. In fact, she had been very good about not looking at it that way. When she thought of Beau, she didn't let her mind stray too far to the man she'd thought he was before he'd tried to buy her. That was the man she'd thought about during sex with Johnny. Just as she'd had his attention, he'd had hers. But that wasn't the man he'd turned out to be. "All I see is what that money could do for our future. I could do this, for us, and it would never mean a thing because *you* are what's important to me."

He was quiet for a few tense seconds. Suddenly, he slammed his fist against the steering wheel.

She bit her lip. "It's not that I want to—"

"I know," he said. "It's not you I'm mad at. It's the situation. It's me."

"You?" He didn't continue. Lola looked at her hands in her lap. She assumed he was mad at himself for even considering the offer, but she was afraid to ask. "Just please tell me what you've been thinking this last week. You've been so hot and cold. I can't figure out what you want, so you have to tell me, and you have to be honest."

Johnny ran a hand over his face and blew out a breath. "You want honesty?"

"Yes."

"I keep thinking about that life," he said. "I want something of my own. We can't live paycheck to paycheck forever, but I don't know how to get out of it. I can't ever seem to catch up."

Lola took his hand again and squeezed it. "I'm relieved that you're also worried. Sometimes I feel like I have to be the one to fix it."

"I want to fix it, Lola, but I don't know how."

Suddenly she wanted to go back to ignoring the problem. She almost wished she hadn't dragged them into this conversation. "Maybe we don't have to," she said. "You'll keep on managing Hey Joe. It won't be the same, but you'll learn to love it. I'll graduate from bar wench to cocktail waitress. Or maybe we get new jobs in a different dive bar. Things would be tight while we transitioned, but they'd settle and we'd get back to where we are now." Lola's voice softened with defeat as she spoke, but she hoped Johnny wouldn't pick up on it.

"Because where we are now is the best option," he said. "You don't think I'll ever be able to give you more than this. Not without someone else's money."

"That isn't what I said."

"You might as well say it. I'll never be more than what I am in this moment."

"I'm trying to be realistic," she said. "If we want more, then I have to do this. If I don't, then this is how things will be. It was enough before Beau came along, but is it enough now? I don't know, Johnny. I don't know the answer to any of this."

He threw open the car door, jumped out and looked back at her. "You want to do this because you think it's our only chance."

Lola also got out of the car. Their doors slammed at the same time. "Don't turn this around on me because I have the guts to say what we're both thinking," she said, hurrying to keep up with him. "This *could* be our only chance. It's not like I want this."

He kept walking.

"I know you want me to do it," she said, raising her voice. "Why don't you man up and tell me the truth?"

He turned around and pointed a finger at her. "You want truth so goddamn bad? The money's all I think about. And the things I could finally do. I'm six-foot-two, two hundred pounds, but I'm half a man because I can't take care of you."

Lola reached for him. "But you do take care of me."

"No, I don't," he said, stepping back. "Five nights a week we get off work while the rest of the world sleeps. We work our asses off, and we're still struggling to get by. If I lose this job, I'll have to start all over somewhere else. I have no other skills. You think you have nothing now? It's about to get a lot worse."

"When did I say I had nothing? Would I like a washer and dryer of my own so I don't have to schlep down the street? Would I like to quit this job one day and try something else? Yes. But that doesn't mean I have nothing. If I do this, it's for the things that *can't* be bought—like our future."

"*If* this, *if* that. I'm tired of this shit. Just make a decision."

"I can't, Johnny," she said, shaking her head. "You have to do it."

"This has to be your choice. I'm not going to send you into another man's bed no matter what I want."

She put her hand to the base of her throat. "Want?" she choked. "Are you saying you *want* me to do this?"

"No," he said. In the dark, their eyes were narrowed on each other. The silence was thick. "I'm saying I won't stop you."

Chapter Six

He slept in bed next to Lola, but Johnny, who was usually unconscious as soon as the lights went out, breathed unevenly. He was awake. He flipped back and forth every few minutes. His mind was elsewhere. They each stayed on their sides of the bed.

It went on for days. When they were alone, he barely looked at her, but she often caught him staring during work. Waiting. For her to bring it up again? For her to make the decision? Did he hope she'd say yes? Or no? His silence meant she had to choose for both of them.

The more silence drew out between them, the more time Lola had alone. Beau was a strong presence in her thoughts. She couldn't forget him in his urbane suit, giving all his attention to whatever he was doing at that moment, whether it was throwing darts, savoring his Macallan—or looking at her. Being near her. Flirting with her. Everything he did, he did a hundred percent.

During a night off, while Johnny worked, Lola finally gave in to her curiosity and looked Beau up online. He hadn't always been wealthy. He'd even grown up twenty minutes from Lola. It was well known that he was a self-made millionaire and that he co-founded Bolt Ventures but had his hand in many different projects. At thirty-seven, he'd never been married, and except for stints here and there, he'd always lived in Los Angeles.

Lola looked for details about him before he'd sold his seventh try at a website, but they were hard to come by. His father had died in a car accident in France. He'd worked part-time jobs and developed his own projects in his spare time, mostly at night.

When she was about to give up, she found one of his first interviews from years earlier. The interviewer had asked what his least favorite job had been before he'd struck it rich. She had to read his answer twice—it was a six-month bartending gig at a hole-in-the-wall place in the Valley. He'd quit because with a thirty-minute commute each way, gas ate into his tips and he wouldn't get home until an unreasonable hour.

Beau had been like them. He hadn't done it for years like she and Johnny, but he'd been in their shoes. He knew struggle. And he'd done what he had to do to get out of it. The question was how far Lola would go to get out of it—and what Beau expected of her if she agreed.

◆ ◆ ◆

The next night, Lola was just about to open the bar

when the phone rang.

"Lola, right?" asked a familiar voice.

"Who's this?"

"Hank Walken. We met last week when I came in to see the space."

"I remember," she said flatly.

"How are you?"

She hadn't expected that question. "Busy," she said. "There something I can help you with?"

"Sure. Got it. Is Mitch around?"

Lola bit her bottom lip and looked toward the backroom. "Not right now," she lied.

"How can I get in touch with him? It's important."

"Try around this time tomorrow. I can get him a message if you want."

"Just tell him to call me, and that time is money. I want this deal worked out in the next forty-eight hours if we can manage it."

"Deal?" Lola asked, her throat closing. She and Johnny had run out of time. It was now or never.

"I told you about the lounge, didn't I?" he asked cheerily. "We'll be looking for pretty, young cocktail waitresses with experience. That's a not-so-subtle hint."

She struggled to register his words. All she could think was that their moment was about to pass them by. "What about management?" she asked, even though she could barely picture herself in a lounge, much less Johnny.

"I like to bring in my own people for the higher-level stuff. Why, you tired of serving?"

"I'm the assistant manager, but I was asking for my

boyfriend. The guy you met."

"Ah." He cleared his throat. "We stick with women on the floor or if we hire males, they're generally models, actors, that kind of thing." He guffawed. "If they can make a drink, even better. But maybe we can find your boyfriend something in the kitchen."

"I'll give Mitch the message," Lola said and hung up.

"Who was that?" Vero asked as Lola walked by her.

"No one." Lola went directly to Mitch's office and closed the door behind her.

He looked up from his paperwork. The radio played The Rolling Stones. "What's up?"

"We're going to make an offer," she said.

He heaved a big sigh. "Lola, I—"

"I just need a little more time."

"Hank won't like that."

She went and set her palms on his desk. Johnny could work anywhere, but he would never be as happy as he was there. She'd been lost once, and Johnny had shown her the way back. Now she'd repay him by giving him what nobody else could. "Johnny's busted his ass for you for over twelve fucking years. He doesn't ask for much. For God's sake, *I've* had to ask for all his raises. You will wait a few more days because you owe him at least that."

Mitch laced his fingers on the desk and looked down. "I just want you to be sure about taking this on. The whole thing could tank if you're not careful."

He had no idea how true that was. "We're sure," Lola said. "We're ready."

"All right," he said, eyeing her up and down. "That's what you want, I'll hold Hank off a few more days."

Lola left Mitch and went into the break room. She leaned against the counter and inhaled a shaky breath. She hoped making the decision would be the hardest part of all. Her stomach was a mix of nerves and anticipation when she thought about the phone call she had to make. She decided Johnny would do it—she already had enough responsibility.

She went back out to the bar. Johnny was mid-pour. Customers at the bar were absorbed in their own conversations.

"I've made my decision," Lola said. "I'll do it."

Johnny didn't look up. He set down the bottle of gin. Now he was the one with a choice to make. If Johnny asked her not to do it right then, she wouldn't. She'd leave Beau in his skyscraper where he belonged. Their worlds had been the same once, and now they'd be the same again. Only, Lola would be the one crossing sides this time. Beau was waiting for her there. One night on his side thrilled her as much as it terrified her, and that was why Johnny needed to tell her not to do it.

Johnny picked up the gin again and continued pouring. "Five hundred isn't enough," he said. His voice was steady but toneless. "We'll ask for more."

◆ ◆ ◆

Beau scrubbed his hand up his jawline and back, looking between Lola and Johnny. Lola couldn't tell in their bare surroundings if Beau was actually solemn, or if he was just reflecting what he saw across the conference table. Even the sky itself had given up the day to gray webs of clouds.

At least he hadn't made them wait. Beau'd walked into the room a couple minutes after the receptionist had shown them in. Lola had watched him round the table, wondering if he'd removed his tie to seem less intimidating or if he'd come into work that day without one. It'd caught her off guard. Suits had never been her thing, but the casual nature of his open collar and exposed neck did something to her, as if she were seeing some forbidden part of him.

Beau was exact with his attention as always. At that moment, he addressed Johnny. "Are you sure you want to be here for this?"

Although reclined in his seat, tension emanated from Johnny. Lola had refused to sit down without him, but first she'd made Johnny promise not to let things get to the level they had last time they'd all been in the same room. "Just get started," Johnny said.

Beau tapped the end of his pen once on the slim folder in front of him. "All right. Half the money will be deposited into your account by five o'clock the night of the arrangement. The other half will come once Lola has held up her end of the bargain."

Beau's formality made Lola's stomach uneasy, but she was grateful for it. She didn't think she could handle anything less tactful. "Exactly what does my end entail?"

"From sunset that night to sunrise the following morning, I own you."

Lola schooled her expression. Inside, her heart was going a mile a minute. If anyone could own a woman, it would be the man sitting in front of her. "You own me," she repeated. "Meaning what?"

Beau put his elbows on the table and played with his pen, twisting the cap. "You're mine to do with what I please, excluding physical harm," he said. "I want to be very clear—I have no intentions of making you physically uncomfortable or of hurting you in any way. This is meant to be a pleasant experience for us both."

Lola was tempted to give Johnny a reassuring look when he shifted in his seat, but she kept her eyes on Beau as if he were a snake that might strike at any time. "Everything else is fair game?" she asked with an unnaturally straight back.

"Aside from anything that puts you at risk, the arrangement ensures that you give me whatever I ask for."

"Not whatever," Johnny said. "There have to be some limits." He looked over at Lola. "There are some things she won't do."

"Johnny," she said under her breath. She refused to go into specifics in a cold, stark conference room with her boyfriend and the man she was about to sleep with sitting across from each other. Johnny was right—she had limits. But she could handle Beau once they were alone.

"We've already covered the limits," Beau said. "To everything else, there's only one answer."

"Yes," Lola said.

Beau nodded once, looking pleased. "Exactly. Just

95

like that."

"How can we trust you won't hurt her?" Johnny asked. His voice was already raised, bordering on aggressive. "Your word doesn't mean dick."

Beau switched back to Johnny and remained calm. "You've probably figured out by now that I'm well known in the business world. I have family members, investors, employees. If anyone's taking a risk, it's me." He pulled a sheet from the folder under his hands and slid it across to Lola. "For that reason, I'll need you both to sign a non-disclosure agreement. There's a clause that if either of us strays from the agreement—including what I just said about physical harm—the NDA is null and void. That's why you can trust me. I've worked long and hard to get where I am. I can't afford to have my name attached to a scandal. My reputation is on the line."

"Then why do this at all?" Lola asked. "Aren't there more discreet ways of buying sex?"

Beau became even more focused on her. He set down his pen. "I'm not buying sex, Lola. I'm buying you. I'd like us to be one hundred percent clear on that. Are we?"

Lola found herself unable to meet his eyes for the first time. Being referred to as an object didn't have the effect she thought it would. Instead of anger, she became acutely aware of the heat between her legs. He could have anyone. He wanted her.

"Are we?" Beau persisted. "If we're not on the same page about that, I need to know now."

She kept her eyes lowered as she looked to the side.

Johnny's head was turned away from her out the window.

"I understand," Lola said.

"Eyes up," Beau said.

Lola swallowed at his curt command. Her gaze traveled over the table's surface, up Beau's crisp, white shirt and its open collar, past his smooth-shaven jaw to his eyes. They were greener than ever with the window's gray backdrop. "You're buying me," she said to him.

"Thank you." His expression relaxed. "But of course there will be sex. For that reason, I'll need you to get tested and bring the results with you the evening of our arrangement."

Johnny snapped back to attention. "Come on, man."

"That's non-negotiable. I'll do the same for you. Without that, there's no deal."

"It's fine," Lola said. "I'll get the tests."

"You have an appointment with my doctor after this," he said. "Are you on birth control?"

Lola took her purse from the floor and set it on the table. She dug inside for her packet.

"I don't need to see it." He held up another piece of paper. "Because while I'd prefer we not have to deal with it at all, this signature absolves me of any responsibility should you get pregnant."

Lola's mouth instantly tingled. It was worse than being treated like an object. Things had happened so fast, she hadn't considered the possibility of pregnancy. Her mind flitted over the past few weeks. She'd been diligent about taking the pill. She leaned over the table and slid the paper toward her.

Johnny sat perfectly still. "I wouldn't worry about the responsibility," he said. "She gets pregnant and I'll kill you. Problem solved."

Lola stared at the paper in front of her, which was only one page, concise and to the point.

"Then we'll make sure that doesn't happen," Beau said. "But I still need Lola to sign it. My lawyers would have heart attacks if they knew I was doing this without them. I prefer not to involve anyone other than us. We can if you'd like, though."

"That won't be necessary." Lola couldn't think too hard about what she was signing or she might lose her nerve.

"If you don't deliver your end of the deal," Beau continued, "I'll be forced to come up with ways of righting the situation. I don't want to resort to that, but I haven't gotten this far in business without doing things I don't like."

"I wouldn't be here if I hadn't thought this through," Lola said.

Beau smiled reassuringly. He looked like he wanted to say something else, but he just squinted at her. "Are you all right?"

Her body had undergone about a hundred different reactions in the last twenty minutes, from shame to arousal to indignation. Was she all right? She couldn't be sure, but she wasn't Beau's responsibility. No matter how much he paid, she would never be his to hold and comfort and reassure. She raised her chin a little. "I'm fine."

"Do you have any questions?"

Johnny moved. "We have demands," he said, rejoining the conversation.

"I thought you might," Beau invited.

"If you don't meet them, we walk right now."

Beau folded his hands on the table. "You have my attention. Proceed."

"We want our half now. Today. And Lola will only do it for eight hundred thousand."

Beau's eyebrows shot up. "Eight hundred? You realize that's sixty percent more than my initial offer?"

"You asked for a counteroffer."

"I did, but this isn't a free-for-all. As with any negotiation, I have my limits."

Johnny shook his head fast. "No. This is the only way we'll do it. Lola's worth more than what you're asking."

Lola resisted jerking her head toward Johnny only because they'd agreed to come in as a unified front. But bringing Lola's worth into the discussion was a low blow.

"Not that she has a price," Johnny backtracked. "What I meant was—"

"I know what you meant," Beau said. "Tread carefully, though. If you push me, I might pull the offer completely."

Johnny shrugged with his whole upper body. Under the table, his leg bounced up and down. "Like I said, she won't do it for a dime less anyway."

"Johnny, relax," Lola said. "You're starting to sound like my pimp."

Johnny's glare at her was brief. Before the meeting, he'd said, "When we get to the money part, let me do the talking." Sweat beaded on his temple despite the blowing air conditioning. Lola, on the other hand, had goose bumps from the cold. Even she wasn't sure if he was bluffing.

When she looked back at Beau, he was watching her, not Johnny. "That's the price you decided on for yourself, Lola?"

"It's not my price," she said. Her mouth soured. The word was as dirty as *worth*. "It's how much we need to buy the bar. The money is useless to us otherwise."

"I really prefer you didn't call my very generous offer useless," Beau said. "Do you have any concept of how much five hundred thousand dollars is?"

"Yes. It's less than eight hundred," Lola said sharply. "You two aren't the only ones who get to blather about worth. If I'm going to degrade myself, it has to be worth it to me, and that means Johnny and I end up with Hey Joe."

"Degrade yourself?" Beau repeated. His laugh was hollow. "I'd say you've already degraded yourself just by taking this meeting."

The nerve. Up until that moment, she'd actually thought he was being fairly decent considering the circumstances. Lola pinched her lips together. "That's not fair. I know you know what it's like to put a dream before everything else."

Beau's smile faded as his face smoothed. "Excuse me?"

"It's not about money or worth. At the end of the

day, Johnny and I are doing this for our future. You killed yourself to make something from nothing—you know what it's like on this side."

"Exactly," Beau said. "You can never understand how hard I've worked to get here, and now I'm offering it to you in exchange for one night. Not even an entire day. You should be on your knees thanking me."

To her embarrassment, she shuddered. The sheer level of her confusion scared her. The more he talked, the angrier she got and the more she wanted to grab his shirt and pull him to her. He seemed to know exactly how to push her buttons, back her into a corner, make her sweat.

"What would you have done in my position?" she asked him.

"Me? Oh, I've sold my soul many times over," he answered. "Now it's my turn to buy."

She stood and steadied herself against the table. "You clawed your way to the top, yet you're still taking advantage of others' desperation. You're depraved. I guess it's true that you can take the person out of the trash, but you can't take the trash out of the person."

He tilted his head. "Is that what they say about you?"

"Go to hell." She didn't have much dignity left, but she wasn't willing to give him every last piece of it. "I can't do this."

The table was silent. She didn't wait to see if Johnny would follow. With one last look at Beau, and a moment of wondering what could've been had she met him at a different time, or maybe even had he not made his offer, but had come back to the bar a second time—with that last look, she walked away.

As soon as she reached the door and her hand was closed around the handle, though, Beau spoke again.

"A million dollars."

It wasn't possible she'd heard him correctly. In her worked-up, jittery state, her mind was playing tricks on her. Beau had no reason to double the amount when he'd been so opposed to eight hundred thousand. She glanced back over her shoulder. Johnny was frozen, his eyes doubled in size.

Beau's fingers were steepled in front of him and the corner of his mouth curled into a slight smile. "One night. One million dollars. And that's my final offer."

Chapter Seven

Johnny cupped Lola's upturned face. He kissed her forehead. "You look terrible."

"That's the plan, isn't it?" With a shaky inhale, she put a smile on her face. Johnny had been surprisingly strong since they'd left Beau's office the day before—for her. She could do the same for him.

"What about the black circles under your eyes?" he asked. "Are they part of the plan?" This time he kissed the top of her head. "You look great to me, anyway. Maybe he won't think so."

Johnny hugged her face to his chest. He'd just gotten out of the shower and smelled like soap. His ratty sneakers sat by the front door next to an empty space where she always left her Converse. Usually their shoes came and went together. She tried to look away, but Johnny held her tightly. She couldn't afford to get sentimental about sneakers. It wasn't like this was the first night they'd ever spent apart.

"I love you," she said. Now that the decision had been made, there was a sense of relief between them, and with that they'd made peace. "We'll get through this."

"I'd never let you go if I thought differently," Johnny said. "It means nothing. I'll go to work like any other night. You'll come home to me in the morning. End of story."

"You forgot the part about how we're a million dollars richer afterward."

"We're already halfway there," he said.

Lola had that fight or flight feeling she always got before a big change in her life. The night she'd started at Hey Joe, she'd begged Johnny to let her go back to her old job and her old friends. At the time, that life had seemed easier than starting over. But even though it was because of Johnny's ultimatum, *she'd* made the decision to leave all that behind. Still, that hadn't meant it was easy.

She looked up at Johnny without pulling away an inch. "We could be in Vegas by midnight. We already have five hundred grand. Start over."

He smiled. "We could take that fake road trip we planned last year. With nowhere to be, it wouldn't matter how long it took. Break out the camping gear—"

A knock on the door interrupted him. Lola squeezed Johnny closer. "I don't want to leave you alone."

"I'll be fine."

"You will?"

He shook his head. "No, but it's only a night, right?

Work will be kind of busy since it's Friday. It'll keep me distracted."

The knock came again.

"Will you check in with Mitch? He can't make any decisions until he hears our offer."

"He'll wait." He pushed a loose strand of her hair behind her ear and kissed her, lingering against her lips. "Lola," he whispered. "Don't kiss him like this. Promise me."

She let him clutch her another moment. She was about to step into a world where she had no jurisdiction over her own body. No matter how badly she wanted to, she couldn't make Johnny that promise. "I'll try."

He tensed when there was more rapping on the door. "Love you too," he said.

Lola was just going to slip out, but Johnny opened the door all the way. On their welcome mat stood a suited man who wasn't Beau, but who didn't look much older than him. He gestured behind him. "Good evening, Miss Winters. I'm Mr. Olivier's driver. He's waiting in the car."

Lola shielded her eyes and followed the man without looking back. At the curb, a limousine idled. As they approached it, the sun disappeared behind the apartment building across the street.

The back window rolled down. Beau's hair was styled in a wave tonight—smoother and darker from product and away from his face. It made his green eyes clearer. He was perfectly put together except for a noticeable layer of stubble. The contrast only added to his appeal.

"Last chance, Lola," he said, looking up at her. He was being playful. "You can still turn around."

She stared, unblinking, unflinching and showed him the papers clutched in her hand. "The tests you requested."

He took them through the window, read them over and smiled. "He's thorough, isn't he?"

"Very." After her tense afternoon with Beau and Johnny in the conference room, Beau's doctor had been kind and gentle with her. He'd even insisted on giving her a check-up.

"Warner, please get the door for Miss Winters."

"Certainly, sir." He stepped past Lola to let her in.

The limo had champagne and other spirits, but champagne was the only thing she could stomach. She sipped it to calm her nerves after reviewing Beau's test results.

"I admire your effort," Beau said, "but it isn't working."

She moved the glass from her mouth. "I'm sorry?"

"Are those Johnny's jeans?"

She looked down at the faded, oversized pants. "Johnny's jeans wouldn't fit me," she said, offended. "They're from Goodwill. It's this place where—"

"I'm familiar with Goodwill, thank you."

She rolled her lips together, pleased she'd hit a nerve. She covered her smile by taking another sip of her drink.

"I'm not buying the act," Beau said. "I know you're intentionally trying to make yourself unattractive."

"Do you always call your dates ugly right off the

bat?"

"I'm saying the opposite, actually. Old jeans and no makeup can't detract from your beauty." He studied her. "But my guess is you already knew that."

Whether she'd known it or not, she couldn't help feeling flattered—even as she reminded herself that in the short time she'd known him, he'd never lacked the ability to charm.

"The only thing I won't let fly is your hair like that," he said.

It was a mild request. She didn't argue. She undid her ponytail, and her hair fell all at once around her shoulders.

"Better," he said.

She looked out the window since the divider had been rolled up, blocking her view of the road. "Are we going to your place?"

"No."

She turned to him. "A hotel?"

"We have a room for the night, yes."

A hotel was good—it meant there'd be people around. "Where is it?"

"Beverly Hills." He paused. "Is that all right with you?"

She'd never stayed in a hotel in Los Angeles since she had no reason to. She'd certainly never stayed anywhere as upscale as Beverly Hills. "Is your house under renovation or something?"

"We'd be more comfortable at a hotel."

Lola looked around the limo. There'd been no mention of where he lived in her research. Her heart plummeted when she realized the most obvious reason he wouldn't want her in his home. She turned back to him.

"I'm not married," he said.

"How'd you know I was going to ask that?"

"I watched it play out on your face," he said. "I like that you're expressive."

She ignored that. "Girlfriend?"

"Completely unattached. I promise."

She wondered if her relief also played out on her face. Beau had chosen *her*, had orchestrated all this for *her*, and if nothing else, Lola would allow herself to feel special about that tonight. The only thing that could take that away would be another woman. "Will we be there soon?"

Beau let her question hang in the air a moment. "Do you want to be there soon?" he asked.

It was a blunt question delivered bluntly. Her answer didn't matter—it wouldn't change the course of her night. It was almost impossible to lie to him, looking as handsome as he did in his tuxedo. He was tall and obviously well built, but was he as hard underneath as he was on the outside? Was he strong? If they had sex against a wall, how long could he hold her up? "No," she said quickly to cover up that last thought. "It all just sounds very top secret."

"It isn't," he said. "You're just asking the wrong questions. We're going to a gala."

"A *what*?" The tuxedo. She'd been so caught up in herself that she hadn't stopped to wonder why he was wearing one.

"A black-tie gala to benefit the L.A. Philharmonic. I needed a date. That's why I picked tonight for us."

She pulled on the hem of her vintage concert tee. "But I'm not dressed for that."

"Thank God you agree. You can wear that if you want, but I prefer not to spend the night looking at Stevie Nicks and her yellow hair."

Lola scrambled. "I wish you'd told me. I can find something more appropriate if you take me back."

"That won't be necessary. I didn't tell you to dress up because I planned a little extra time for shopping."

"I didn't realize...I thought we would just—"

"Fuck?"

Lola's breath caught. If Johnny ever spoke to her that way, it wasn't in broad daylight, outside the heat of the moment. "Honestly," she said, swallowing back her surprise, "it wouldn't take me long to run into my apartment. I only have one dress that would—"

"I'd be a madman to take you back now that I have you."

Lola shut her mouth. He was becoming bolder, catching her off guard more. "You will, though, won't you?" she asked quietly, not entirely sure he'd say yes. "Take me home?"

"In the morning, as promised. But not a minute sooner." He moved the test results from between them to the floor and placed his arm along the back of the seat. "First we'll go shopping. You'll wear what I select for you, and I'll pay for it."

"I'm not comfortable with that. It's not part of the deal. I can buy my own clothing."

He zapped her conviction with a look. "In case it needs to be reiterated, Lola, I always say what I mean. Nothing is open to discussion. And since you've promised yourself over to me for the next twelve or so hours, make this easy for us both and comply."

"If you were looking for a woman who'd just comply, I don't think I'd be here right now."

His eyes narrowed. "What makes you say that?"

"A man like you would have no problems finding willing women. You want someone unwilling. Someone you have to work for. You think I'm trashy, maybe a little wild, and that does something for you. I understand." For the first time since she'd met Beau, Lola felt in control. The look on his face and the quickening of his breath gave him away. He leaned into her as if he didn't even realize he was doing it. "If you tell me exactly what you're looking for," she said, "I can play that part for you. I've done it before."

"You've done what before?" he asked, hardly even blinking.

"Been someone's fantasy."

"Not their reality, though." He'd slid over in the seat, far enough that he'd have to reach to kiss her, but still close.

"No."

"I want the reality. You. Just you."

She lifted one shoulder. "You have me. My body's already yours. If it's not enough, tell me what to be."

"I made myself clear on this already. This is about you, Lola. Not just what's underneath those jeans and T-shirt. I won't accept anything less than everything from you tonight."

She shook her head coyly. "My body is one thing, the rest of me is another. What you paid for is only what's underneath these jeans and T-shirt."

The car slowed to a stop. Beau straightened up abruptly. "You're wrong. That's not what we agreed on." He looked away from her and opened the door before the driver could.

Lola took Beau's hand and unfolded out of the car. Palm trees framed the tall windows of the marble storefront, which displayed smartly dressed mannequins. "I hate to tell you this," Lola said, "but these shops are closed."

He put his hand on her upper back, trapping the ends of her hair. "Not for us," he said, guiding her forward. The brass-handled, glass doors opened with his words.

"You must be Lola," said a slick-haired blonde saleswoman, outstretching her hand. "I understand it's an important night for you."

Another woman appeared with two glasses of champagne.

"Is that what he told you?" Lola asked, taking a drink.

"Lola," Beau warned. "Don't pretend your thirtieth birthday dinner is just another night."

The saleswoman smiled. "Well, you're in good hands with us." Both women disappeared somewhere into the pristine, bone-and-black-lacquer interior.

"It's not even close to my birthday," Lola said. "Why the subterfuge?"

"It's fun to watch you squirm."

"Well, if we're playing games, could I not be thirty already? How would you like if I went around telling people you're forty when you're not for a few more years?"

How he smiled at that, crooked-lipped and dimple-deep—as if it were the best thing he'd heard in a while. "Did a little research on me, I see."

"Don't be flattered—"

"I wouldn't dream of it."

"It was only to make sure you weren't wanted for murder or something. I'm still not entirely convinced you aren't."

"Well." His smile only widened. "I'm glad you decided to put your life in my hands anyway. Funny how a little money turns the other cheek."

She followed Beau to the back of the store, frustrated at her lack of comeback.

He stopped at a clothing rack. "Here are the things I've preselected. I'd like to see them all on you."

"For one evening?" She balked at the price tag. "Some of these cost more than my month's rent." She flipped it over. "Make that two months."

"While you're with me, you'll be dressed the part— every hour, every minute." He took her champagne glass from her. "I'll refill your drink. You can change around the corner."

She picked up the first dress and took it to the fitting room, holding it away from her as though it might break. It was lovely and expensive. She hated it. The high neck and gathered fabric along one side was completely out of line with her taste.

Just as she'd stripped down to her underwear, he knocked. She glanced at the door. Beau might be proving difficult to decode, but Lola was sure about one thing—he liked power. Control. He fed on weakness—in a single bite—and it made him stronger.

Lola wasn't weak, though. She'd let Beau do the biting, but just enough to keep him satisfied and no more. It'd been a while since she'd had the attention of a man like Beau, but she had, and she hadn't forgotten this game.

Lola opened the door wide. She slid her hand up along the edge and cocked her hip just enough for him to notice. "You knocked?"

He schooled his expression in one quick second, but not before Lola caught his surprise. His slow gaze drifted down her neck, past her wide-strapped, sea-foam-green bra, over her naked stomach to her mismatched, oversized panties.

"Stubborn right down to her underwear," Beau said, more amused than annoyed.

"It's laundry day." Lola shrugged. "My less modest things are—well, probably in Johnny's hands as we speak since it's his week to do the wash."

"Good thing they carry lingerie here," he said, less amused.

"Oh, don't waste another dollar on me. I'm fine with this if you are."

He smiled thinly. "I'm not. As I said, you're to dress the part every hour, every minute. That includes our time alone." He passed her a fresh glass of

113

champagne. "I'll take care of it, but for now, I'll be outside your door. Talk to me while you change."

She shut herself into the fitting room and went to lock it but didn't bother. If Beau wanted to come in, he would. Wouldn't he? It'd been almost an hour and he hadn't made any move to touch her yet. When he did, would she like it? Could she enjoy being touched by Beau when she loved someone else? She shivered and passed her hands over her biceps. "What do you want to talk about?"

"Have you ever been here?"

"Rodeo Drive? Sure." She removed the dress gingerly from the hanger. Despite her feelings about it, it was still a beautiful piece of clothing. "Mostly to walk around. Truth be told, it isn't really my style."

"No, I don't suppose there's a lot of leather here."

"You don't like the leather?" she asked, smiling a little to herself.

"I didn't say that. What are you doing now?"

She looked down. "Pulling on the dress."

After a moment, he asked, "How about now?"

"The dress is tight, so it's taking a minute to get on. What are you doing?"

Beau laughed. "Well, now I'm picturing you struggling with a tight dress. Something I look forward to seeing later."

"Later?" Lola had expected to be in his bed by now, but his behavior bordered on gentlemanly. Curiosity urged her closer to the door. "Not now?"

He didn't respond right away. "No," he said. "Now I'm using my imagination."

"Can I ask you why without you taking it the wrong way?"

"Which way would be the wrong way?"

Absentmindedly, she touched the doorframe with a finger. "Not that I want this or that I'm trying to provoke you." She carefully considered what she was trying to say. "But how come you haven't done anything yet? You do know we only have tonight?"

"Tonight will be over before we both know it," he said. "That may be good news for you, but I intend to unwrap you slowly so I don't miss anything." He paused. "If you were worried about me breaking into your dressing room and bending you over the bench...you can relax."

Lola's eyes went directly to the bench. If he bent her over it, she'd be face to face with herself in the mirror. She'd see everything—like Beau behind her in his tuxedo. She closed her eyes, willing away the warmth seeping through her. Things were not supposed to be this way. Her plan was only to endure his weight on top of her, not anticipate it. Not enjoy it.

"Are you all right?" he asked. "You've been quiet for some time."

She cleared her throat and moved away from the door. "I'm fine."

"What are you doing now?"

"Unfastening my bra."

"How come?" he asked.

"It's the wrong kind. Should be racerback." There was a weighty pause. "Now I'm zipping up the dress."

"What's the material?"

"Silk, I think. It must be silk."

"Why do you say that?"

"It's smooth and soft," she said. "It feels…"

"Yes?"

"Silky."

"You can't see, but I'm smiling. Can I come in now?"

She opened the door.

Beau stood from his chair. "Beautiful."

"Thanks."

"But purple doesn't suit you."

"I hate purple."

"What color do you like?" he asked.

"Black."

"I should've known."

She left the room, went around the corner and past the rack of Beau's selections. Something near the front had caught her eye when she'd walked in. She found it in her size and returned to the fitting room, where Beau remained in the same spot, watching her. Behind the door again, she was alone. "Beau?"

"Yes, Lola?"

Alone with his voice.

"Why me?" she asked.

She put the purple dress back on its hanger while he took his time responding. "I suppose I should've been prepared for this question."

"You could just be honest," she suggested.

"All right. It started with the first moment I saw you. Everything else just…ceased to exist. Time. People. Music. You stood there like a prize waiting to be claimed. It stopped me in my tracks."

Jesus. Had he claimed her yet? Or was that to come? Her face flushed as if she were back outside the bar, having just put a dent in a teenager's car with her tennis shoe. "That's who I am."

"Who are you?"

"The girl you saw that night. I'm not expensive silk dresses and Friday-night events. I'm just the scrappy kid I always was, a girl who's made some bad decisions, good ones too. Nothing special."

"That's not what I saw," Beau said. "I saw confidence, resistance, strength. Blue, bloodthirsty eyes."

The girl Beau described reminded Lola of herself when she was younger. She was still that girl, just not as vibrantly as she'd been back then. "Will you zip me?" she asked.

She opened the door and turned to face the dressing room mirror. The black floor-length gown had two straps that came around her neck and dipped in the front. Soft, pebbled leather subtly trimmed the neckline.

Beau appeared at her back. In one hand, she held up her hair. He didn't touch her once while he raised the zipper. Their eyes caught in the reflection. "This is the dress," he said. "I don't need to see any others."

"You certainly know what you like, don't you?" she asked.

They stared at each other. Slowly, he lowered his mouth to the curve of her shoulder. His stubble lit instant chills over her skin. She inhaled deeply, quietly. Her lids fell more with each careful, sensual kiss—along

117

her neck, under her ear, on her cheek. She wet her lips and parted them for him.

"Not yet," he said in her ear.

"When?" she breathed.

"Soon. You aren't ready for me. I hope you are at some point, but either way, it will be soon." He held her gaze. "You asked me why you? I'm drawn to you in a way that can't be ignored for long. There are limits to my patience." He backed away. "Wait here," he said before disappearing.

It was a moment before she dropped her hair. His restraint surprised her more than anything else so far.

Her eyes fell to her faux-leather brown hobo-style purse slumped in the corner. It looked out of place even on the floor, which was plush, white carpet. She glanced over her shoulder then squatted and retrieved her phone to text Johnny.

Everything's fine. We're just shopping. Going to an event.

She put the phone back right before Beau entered the room with a saleswoman loaded down with shoes, jewelry and a clutch that matched the dress. She put everything on the bench above Lola's purse.

Beau also had something for her in his hands, and he was clearly anticipating her reaction.

She took the lingerie from him without flinching. "It's lovely," she said. She ran a finger over the fine lace corset and then checked the price tag. "But is it necessary? I've never spent this much on anything and certainly not to sleep in."

"It's more necessary than anything else we buy tonight," Beau said in a deeper voice than usual. "And you won't be sleeping in it."

The saleswoman visibly bumbled as she left the room.

Lola's phone chimed behind her, and Beau's eyes cut to her purse. "Perhaps I didn't make myself clear. Tonight you belong to me. And *no*. Not just your body." He went and picked up her bag, pulled out the phone and read the screen. "Your thoughts and your heart too." He slipped it into his pocket. "As long as you're with me, *he* doesn't exist."

Her mouth hung open a little. "I'm sorry if you thought any amount of money would get you my heart," she said.

He stepped close to her. Mint cooled the champagne on his breath. "When it comes to which parts of you I own, don't fucking challenge me again. Is that understood? I own them all. Period." He took a deep breath, but it didn't seem to calm him. "There's still five hundred grand on the line. Act like you want to be here with me, or I'll call everything off."

She held his glare, trying to manage her own temper. She wouldn't walk away now. Beau was regaining his hold on her, like the one he'd had the night they met. Giving all of herself over wasn't an option, though—not if she wanted anything back when this was over.

"What's it going to be?" he asked. With another step, his shirt ghosted against her nipples. "Keep the half a mil and walk right now, or give yourself to me until I say stop?"

"I asked you why me," she said. "Your answer was that you're drawn to me. I don't believe you."

"What do you believe?"

"That you have to pay women for their attention," she said. She didn't believe that at all, but his composure was unnerving, and she craved a real reaction.

"You looked me up. You saw the endless buffet of women I have to choose from."

"You're a pig," Lola said. "A buffet? You think of women as food?"

He licked his lips quickly, reached up and brushed her hair away from her neck. "Those women are a buffet. But you? You're a delicacy. I'll eat you slowly with attention to every bite. I'll drink you like fine wine, savoring your taste, inhaling your scent, letting you own me for as long as you're in my mouth."

Lola exhaled an unintentional noise.

"I'll swallow all of you, but you won't realize it until it's too late. Until you're a part of me," he said. "That's what you sold me. That's what I paid for."

It would've been enough to frighten any other woman. It should've sent her sprinting back into Johnny's arms. The idea of being consumed by Beau did scare Lola, but it excited her more.

She didn't know whether to kiss him or back away, but it didn't matter. He was already leaving the room. "Put the things you wore here in the shopping bag by the door," he said over his shoulder. "Everything else in this room should be on your body tonight."

Chapter Eight

It took three technicians to turn Lola inside out. She was transformed. After their visit to the boutique, Beau's next stop had been a nearby salon. Within an hour, her hair had been washed, dried and swept into a loose updo, and her makeup flawlessly applied. Her nails were the color of sweet cherries. Lola watched raptly as the makeup artist carefully glided on the final touch—vivid lipstick, also cherry, also sweet.

"Everything else will catch his attention," the woman said quietly as she worked, "but this will be his undoing."

Lola wanted to explain that she didn't care if Beau was undone or not but her lips were occupied. Beau was never far away, and now he watched her in the mirror. There was no question he liked what he saw. And she liked that he liked it.

Maybe Lola did care if he was undone. After all, no matter how hard she fought her attraction, he was still a man and she was still a woman.

A fact she was reminded of with every movement. The corset Beau had picked out was not just an undergarment—it was a promise of things to come. The stiff, black lace kept her nipples at attention. It straightened her back, bared her while concealing her. It said, *Always be delectable for whoever might look.*

Underneath, black stockings, trimmed also with lace, stopped at the tops of her legs. When she rubbed her thighs together in the chair, the sheer parts felt silky, the lace parts coarse.

She hadn't shown this much cleavage in years, and she found it ironic that even then it had been a form of survival.

When Beau approached the chair, everyone else faded instantly away.

"People have a habit of disappearing around you," she said.

"They know what I want."

Lola looked at his reflection. "And what's that?"

"Privacy." He frowned. "I told them to leave your hair down."

"I told them to put it up." She uncrossed her legs. "It suits the dress."

"I don't care about the dress. I only care what suits me."

"You don't like it?" she asked.

"I suppose." He took one of the loose strands that framed her face between his fingers. "There'll be plenty of time for me to do what I want with it later."

Seated, Lola came up to Beau's chest. The mirror

framed them like a photograph. All made up, Lola finally looked as though she belonged by his side. "Beau," she said, "there are things you don't know about me."

"I imagine quite a few."

"It's not just that Rodeo Drive isn't my taste. I also don't belong here."

"Says who?"

"You think I do?" she asked, mostly to hear what he'd say.

He was no longer looking in her eyes. She followed his gaze to her mouth. "I think you should only care about one person's opinion," he said. "Mine. I don't know who belongs where, but in my eyes, you're a queen among peasants wherever you go."

Lola stammered for a response. It shouldn't have surprised her that Beau was attracted to her—he'd made himself clear on that point—but he still hadn't given her a reason she could grasp. "Thank you," she said lamely.

He looked up again. "In my office, you made a speech about how we have similar pasts, but now we're on different sides. When you grow up on one side, though, you can never really cross over to the other. If you don't belong here, neither do I."

"Don't you ever feel out of place?"

"If I do, I don't let it show. I fake it. People will believe anything if you do it with confidence." He checked his watch. "Come. It's time to go."

The limo idled out front. Her personal effects were taken from her. She didn't care. Nothing had ever felt as good on her body as the things Beau had bought her.

"The rules apply even more so in public," Beau said as they drove away from the salon. "You're with me. Only me. Act as though it were true."

"Will there be press there?"

"Yes. Let them speculate. A beautiful woman like you won't go unnoticed, and I don't want you to."

Lola had the looks to back up her swagger, but Los Angeles was a hub for beautiful people. She doubted she'd get much attention amongst its upper crust. "Why not?" she asked.

"There are people who doubt my business practices because I'm...how do I put it? Social."

"You sleep around."

He gave her a sidelong glance. "Actually, no."

She pushed his shoulder with her fingertips. "You're such a liar. You must think I'm dense or blind. Women probably trip over themselves for a shot with you."

Beau raised one eyebrow. "You didn't. If you tripped at all, it was while running in the opposite direction."

She lowered her head a little as she smiled. "That's because I have a—" She stopped herself.

"So if you didn't have a—"

"You're trying to change the subject." Beau was undoubtedly a catch, enough to make Lola wonder why he was still single. He had to have known things would be different between them without Johnny in the picture. It was one of those things better left unsaid, though. "Anyway, you were lying about how women aren't all over you."

124

"I didn't say that at all." He winked playfully. "But just because a woman wants me doesn't mean she gets me. I'm selective. First, I choose the woman."

"That's it?" she asked.

"Of course not. I have to get her to choose me back."

"Who wouldn't choose you back?" Lola hadn't thought before she spoke, which meant she was becoming too comfortable. She sat up straighter, leaning slightly back from him.

Beau tilted his head, studying her as if she were a science project. "In my experience, not many," he said. "In any case, I don't sleep with every woman I'm photographed with. Sometimes a photo is just a photo."

"It doesn't matter either way to me," she said quickly. She changed the subject. "I'm not one of those girls, so I don't think I understand my role tonight."

"My being unmarried doesn't make me more of a risk, but some people see it that way. I don't make a habit of kowtowing to that kind of thing unless it affects my business, which it's beginning to. It's been four months since I've been in public with anyone. There's speculation I've settled down. Might as well let them think you're the reason for that."

"So I'm the one you've 'settled down' with?" He was asking her to be herself. Instead of his sex object, now she was a person. It wasn't quite what she'd expected from the night. "How do I be that if we've only just met?"

"Only give them your first name. A little mystery is good. Don't answer anything personal. I don't want your bar, your past or your partner associated with me."

Lola's confidence took a hit. "If I embarrass you, why even bring me at all?"

"Ah," he said softly, as if comforting her. "It takes a great deal to embarrass me, Lola. I said that for your protection. The press has no regard for anyone. If they see you with me, then suddenly what I do affects you. Best if we can limit that to one night."

He wanted to protect her? More and more he was uncharacteristically gentlemanly. There was a very small possibility her assumptions about a man who offered money for sex were wrong. Maybe he wasn't completely soulless. Maybe there was more to him than money and expensive suits. Lola thawed. She couldn't think of anything to add, so she just said, "He has a name, you know."

"Who?"

"Johnny. The way you say *partner* sounds sterile."

Beau didn't respond. He seemed more interested in what was out the window.

◆ ◆ ◆

Beau's limo door opened, and camera flashes blinded Lola. He offered her his hand. She only took it to be polite, but the noise, the brightness, the desperation crowding in on them—they were the reasons she didn't let go.

Photographers called for him. They called for them together. They ordered her out of the picture, and Beau's grip on her hand became crushing.

She smiled in every direction. The rolled-out carpet matched her nail polish. Behind them, a vinyl wall advertised the L.A. Philharmonic and the event's sponsor, Rolex. At one point, there were A-list celebrities to her left and right. When she got her bearings navigating both the carpet and the press in towering shoes, she tried to pull her hand away. Beau kept it tightly in his. "Don't," he whispered and kissed her cheek. "I'm the one holding on to you."

Whether he'd meant it or it was for show, hearing that made her a tinge protective of him. The media was made up of too many toothy smiles to count, and in the glaring lights, they became a unit. A snarling beast, hungry for Beau.

An entertainment channel reporter had caught his kiss. "Beau? Beau!" she cried from the other side of the velvet rope. Even with her teased, platinum hair that added a couple inches, she barely came up to Lola's shoulder. In a leopard-print dress, the woman was about as opposite of Lola as it came. "Kissing in public?" She gasped. "Does this mean it's serious?"

Beau slid his arm around Lola's waist. She had to give him credit. There were practically stars in his eyes when he turned to her and said, "Very."

The reporter's gaze flickered over Lola without touching her face. "Who is she?"

Suddenly, Lola and Beau were no longer on different sides. Beau wasn't these people. He looked her in the eye when he spoke to her. He didn't talk over her or tell her to move out of the way. She craned her head to the microphone in Beau's face. "*She* is Lola."

The reporter pouted, touching Beau's forearm. "Oh, dear. Hearts are breaking around the nation. Does this mean the chance to snag the handsome Beau Olivier has passed?"

Something flared in Lola seeing the woman's long red fingernails on him. Beau had chosen Lola tonight, not whoever was under the putrid cloud of hairspray and perfume in front of them. "That's exactly what it means," Lola said. "So kindly remove your claw from my man."

The reporter finally looked at Lola with such lit-up indignation, Lola had to suck in her cheeks to keep from laughing.

"Lola," Beau said.

She swallowed her laugh. She'd had no right to say it. Beau didn't belong to her. It shouldn't bother Lola that the woman looked and acted cheap, thinking that did anything for Beau. Maybe it *did* do something for him.

Lola was appropriately sheepish as she looked up and met his glinting eyes. When he spoke, it was for her and no one else. "Patience has never been my strong suit," he said, drawing her front flush against his, "but I do take credit for resisting this long."

He caught her mouth with his. Their lips pressed together hard, the way his hand pressed the nape of her neck. Her palm went automatically to his chest. He was solid under her hand, just as his arm was solid around her. Camera flashes exploded like fireworks. When his fingers coiled into her neck and her hip, her body stirred, prickling with warmth, as if waking up from a long sleep. She was acutely aware of being so tightly against the hard length of him. She angled her head up to deepen the kiss right before he pulled back.

His expression almost seemed to ask permission, overdue though it was. People shouted at them, but it quickly became white noise.

"Your lips are red," she said.

"So are yours."

Deliriously, she laughed at the thought that they wore the same lipstick. She placed her hands on his cheeks and wiped the red away with her thumbs.

"I have a handkerchief," he said.

"We don't use handkerchiefs where I come from."

"That's okay. I think I like your way better."

She ended up smearing it over her hands and his face. "I'm making it worse."

He laughed. "Not for me. How about we clean up and get a drink?"

The reporter studiously avoided them by trying to get someone else's attention. "You read my mind," Lola said.

Getting anywhere proved difficult. People stopped Beau every few steps. They each patted their mouths with Beau's handkerchief as a temporary fix. He held her hand. She let him. What choice did she have? Her hand, and all her other parts, belonged to him in that moment. When Beau turned away from her, Lola touched her fingertips to her lips. She doubted a single camera had missed their display. Johnny might see it.

"You okay?" Beau looked at her hand at her mouth.

"Your scruff tingles," she said. "You'd think someone going on a million-dollar date would have the decency to shave."

"I'll shave tonight if you want. Before bed."

Before bed. As if they were an old married couple who never spent a night apart. The tingling became stronger as she thought about the fact that his mouth would be on her again and soon—*before bed.* "I didn't say I minded," she said softly, her face upturned to him.

He grunted or something, a deep noise of approval as his eyes jumped between her lips and eyes. "You know just the right things to say, don't you? I have unfairly high expectations of people, yet somehow you continue to exceed them."

"And here I was trying to be less than expected," she said, but she was teasing him. The gap she'd insisted on keeping between them was closing the more comfortable she became. "You do put on a pretty good show."

He shook his head slowly. "What show?"

"Holding my hand, kissing me for the cameras? You're sending a message all right."

"If I am, that doesn't have to mean it's a show. I believe you're mine and no one else's. I meant what I said to that reporter—tonight, it's very serious."

Lola wanted to stay skeptical. It was easier that way. Beau didn't have her completely convinced there was good somewhere underneath his suit, but she was beginning to doubt it was all bad.

"What are you having tonight?" he asked.

Well vodka with club soda was her go-to drink, but

she stopped her automatic response just in time. She wasn't that girl tonight. "Dirty martini," she said. "Grey Goose, please."

Beau ordered for them. She no sooner took the drink than Beau was approached once again, this time by a sturdy, red-cheeked man just as tall as Beau but many years older. "Evening, Olivier," he said, shaking Beau's hand. "Nice to see you."

"You as well, sir." Beau turned slightly. "This is Lola, my date for the evening—"

"It's been a while, hasn't it? I haven't seen you at one of these things with anyone lately."

"I wish I could say your concern with my personal life is flattering."

"Oh, you know I'm messing with you," he said, slapping Beau on the back. "You can't expect an old, married guy like me not to want to live vicariously. You always have a beautiful woman on your arm."

Lola hadn't been ignored by any man this much since she'd grown breasts. Even Beau had turned away from her. "I prefer you don't talk about me as if I'm not standing right here," she said.

Beau smiled a little and shook his head, but the man turned to face her completely. "Well, shoot. I'm sorry, darling. Where are my manners?"

"I was wondering the same thing about everyone here," Lola said.

His laugh was more of a guffaw. "Well, aren't you a breath of fresh air from Beau's usual type?"

Beau frowned. "Excuse me?"

"She's the first—" He stopped to address Lola.

131

"You might be the first of Beau's dates I've ever heard speak."

"Perhaps you should be thankful for that," she said.

More merry laughing—the man was quickly becoming besotted with her. "I am. I certainly am."

Beau, on the other hand, narrowed his eyes. "Come on, now. What'd those girls ever do to you two?"

"They had something that was mine," Lola practically cooed, batting her lashes with exaggeration. "In case you hadn't noticed, I'm very possessive of my things."

Beau smoothed his hand down his tuxedo shirt. "I hadn't, actually."

Lola raised one eyebrow, waiting for Beau's bantering response, but nothing came.

"Lola," the man said, calling her attention away, "are you as good at keeping Olivier in line as you are me?"

She turned away from Beau and winked. "Better."

He nodded high with his chin in the air. "I'm impressed."

"Does this mean you'll take the meeting?" Beau asked, his wits seemingly recovered.

"Let's not worry about business right now. Listen, a spot opened up at my table—why don't you two join me there tonight?"

"We'd be honored, Mayor Churchill," Beau said. "Table one, is it?"

"That's right. See you there."

"*Mayor*?" Lola asked, gaping as he walked away.

Beau smiled. "Did I not mention that?"

"Oh, God. I didn't recognize him." Lola covered her face. "I was just incredibly rude to the mayor of Los Angeles."

Beau laughed, pulling her hands away. "He was incredibly rude to you, but that's my fault. I bring it out in him."

She shook her head. "I need to learn to keep my big mouth shut."

"Please don't," he said. "I love not knowing what will come out of it next. Such as the charming way you called me a *thing* after the fit you threw over my buffet comment."

"I said what?" Lola asked.

"Just now you said you were very possessive of your *things*."

"That's hardly the same. You referred to women as something you can pick up next to a tub of fried chicken," Lola said. "I was just playing nice for your friend like you wanted. Has he ever invited you to his table before?"

Beau pursed his lips. "No."

"Then I must've done something right."

"You did something to me, at least." He scanned her face. "I like you being possessive over me."

"I'm not. I was just doing what you asked."

He sipped something dark from his glass and surveyed the room. "I'm not sure why you continue to fight this. The deal's been made, but truth be told, I think you want to be here. You just won't admit it."

She studied his profile. There was a disconnect in

his eyes, as if not looking at her meant she wasn't there. It made him darker. It occurred to her just how much power he had tonight. He'd treated her like glass so far, but he could still shatter her with a flick of his wrist. "Beau? What if I decide not to go through with this?"

He blinked once and turned his head to her. When he raised his hand, she flinched. He touched his thumb to the corner of her lips. "You know what our arrangement is," he said. His voice dropped. "And on one point I've been very clear. Until sunrise, you're mine."

His thumb was still pressed against her skin, distracting her. "I know self-defense," she said.

"You won't need it." He shook his head. "Trust me."

Had she met Beau another time, a time when Johnny wasn't part of her life, she would've been attracted to him. He wasn't her type—Johnny was, with his unsmoothable edges and no-bullshit attitude. His faded hair, faded tattoos, faded black T-shirts. Beau's dark-brown hair was just enough for her to grab a handful and no more. Lola had an eye for expensive things even if she didn't own any, and nothing on Beau's body came cheap. He just beat Johnny in height, but where Johnny's T-shirts stretched across his torso, Beau's terse suits—and tuxedos—perfectly complemented his broad shoulders and muscular, lean frame.

"My eyes are up here," Beau teased.

She blinked up from his chest. "Sorry."

"Where'd you go?"

She just shook her head.

"Look," Beau said, sighing, "we have an agreement, yes, but I'm not resting on that. I'm obviously attracted to you or you wouldn't be here." He paused. "Maybe I don't need that reciprocated, but I want it. And I'm willing to work for it."

"I love my boyfriend," Lola said. "You can't expect me to enjoy sleeping with you."

"I do expect it," Beau said. "When I make love to you tonight, it'll be in a way that demands everything from you."

Lola's throat tightened. Nowhere in their arrangement had they said they'd be making love. This was just supposed to be sex—straight up sex. No romance. No fantasy. Definitely no lovemaking.

"I wouldn't pay a million *pennies* for any other woman," Beau continued. "This is about you, not me. Tonight, you're my queen." He made sure she was looking him in the eye when he added, "And that makes me your king. If you're worried about making love, don't be. I'm going to fuck you too."

Lola covered her mouth but couldn't tear her eyes away from him. "Beau," she said behind her hand.

"I don't want any misconceptions. I'm going to make you uncomfortable. I'm going to worship you. I'm going to dominate you. Any man who just has sex with a woman like you is a fool. I want to make art with you—dirty, impossible, fucked-up, beautiful art."

Lola's mind reeled. The image he'd painted was too vivid to shut out. There were people all around them, but inside she was tightly wound and aching for him to untwist her. One hand twitched with the urge to slap him while the other wanted to fist his lapel and bring him closer.

"Now you're giving me something," Beau said, watching her with intensity. "Something I can work with."

Lola didn't even know the skin she was in. "I need to fix my lipstick. I can meet you at the table."

He straightened up. "Go ahead. I'll wait."

Lola rushed to the nearest bathroom and stood in front of the mirror. Only the slight flush of her cheeks gave her away. The reality of the situation hit her. She would be having sex with this man—this *stranger*. It was no longer about money, but about two people spending the night together. Her heart pounded from Beau's words. She could feel blood circulating through her for the first time ever.

It wasn't Beau's promise of things to come that scared her anymore. Nor was it his threat that it was too late to change her mind. What scared her was wanting this, and at the idea of being fucked by him, she had.

She took out the lipstick the makeup artist had given her. She didn't leave the bathroom until it was applied perfectly.

Beau noticed. "You look composed again," he said when she returned.

Lola hated that word. Only people with something to hide composed themselves. But he was right—she was struggling to be herself in an environment so obviously meant for someone else.

They were the last ones to the dining table. After

introductions had been made, Beau put his mouth to Lola's ear and said, "Mayor Churchill is one of those who equates my inability to commit to one woman with the way I do business. An invitation to his table is an opportunity."

His warm breath pebbled her skin. She nodded to show she understood, but with him so close, her mind was back on their kiss. It'd been so convincing that even she'd believed it. There had been need and desire in the way his hands had gripped her, but something gentler and almost reverent in his lips.

Beau conversed easily with the table, but Lola wasn't listening. She watched. He had an unnerving way of focusing on whoever was speaking. It was similar to how he'd approached Lola and Johnny with his proposition. Where did business end with him? Would it carry over into the bedroom?

"So, Lola," Mayor Churchill said between dishes, "are you from Los Angeles?"

Beau took her hand under the table.

"Not too far from here, Mayor Churchill," she said. "East Hollywood."

"Same here," he said proudly. "In fact, the only thing Beau and I have in common is pulling ourselves up by the bootstraps. And call me Glenn."

"We have more in common than that," Beau said.

"Do we?" Glenn asked, smiling as he cut his chicken.

"We both love the city we grew up in and want to do right by it." Beau nodded at Lola. "We both appreciate beautiful women."

137

Glenn waved his fork in their direction. "Okay, you got me there."

"Did Beau mention how we met?" Lola asked.

"Why don't you tell me," Glenn invited.

Beau went tense beside her, his hand tightening around hers.

"First you have to suspend disbelief long enough to picture Beau in a dive bar," she said.

"A dive bar?" Glenn laughed. "What, in his Prada suit and tie?"

"Exactly," Lola said. "We met under some neon signs on the Sunset Strip."

Glenn sat back in his seat. "I haven't been out on the Strip at night in years. In high school, we'd volunteer to post flyers for shows all over Hollywood so the bars would let us in to watch."

Lola grinned. Her instinct that Glenn would get the story looked right. "Have you been to Hey Joe?"

"Have I been there? I passed out in my own vomit on Hey Joe's bathroom floor before you kids were even born." He sighed heartily. "Those were the days," he muttered before glancing quickly around the table. "Don't repeat that."

"That part of the Strip might not be much these days," Lola said, "but Beau and I met there over Scotch and a show." She reasoned the night had been such a spectacle, it counted as a kind of show.

"I almost can't picture it," Glenn said. "Is it true, Olivier?"

"The place is legendary," Beau said warily.

Lola leaned over and kissed Beau's cheek. "For

more reasons than one, now," she said loud enough for Glenn to hear.

"Ever see any good bands there?" someone asked the mayor.

"That was risky," Beau whispered as the conversation steered away from them.

"What, the kiss?" Lola asked, knowing perfectly well what he meant.

He shook his head slowly. "The kiss I didn't mind. It was a nice touch." He rubbed his thumb over her knuckles and pulled her hand from her lap to his. That simple movement gave her a rush of adrenaline. Her hand was so close to him and still not nearly as close as it would be soon.

"What are you thinking about?" Beau asked.

It was written all over his face that he knew exactly what she was thinking. Churchill still talked about his days on the Sunset Strip, so she took his cue. "I was thinking about all the shows I've seen."

"I'll bet you've seen a lot."

She nodded. "In high school, I snuck into bars all the time for live music, usually with a bad boy whose life's mission was to get me drunk." Her eyes drifted over Beau. "That's always been my type. I never dated anyone who wore a suit."

"You're mistaken if you think only good boys wear suits."

Lola nearly lost her heart to her stomach. Bad boys had always been her thing, but since meeting Beau, she was more and more drawn to the suit. She hated to think how she'd fare faced with a combination of the two. "You're teasing me."

"Maybe." He grinned. "Maybe not."

"I don't exactly think you were an angel, but I can't picture you as rebellious."

"I was in the chess club."

Lola laughed loudly. She didn't care that people looked over at them—she was too delighted by the news. "So you were a geek."

"Chess isn't geeky. It taught me the importance of strategy, and," he paused and pulled her hand even farther into his lap, "how to manipulate the pawns in my favor."

She ignored his insinuation. "Were you any good?"

"No, thankfully."

She wrinkled her nose. "What? Why thankfully?"

"We learn far more from defeat than victory, Lola. Every loss means an opportunity to become better. Stronger. I didn't know it then, but I was preparing for the challenges that would come my way. It's made me a better businessman. And a formidable opponent."

"Opponent?" she asked.

"At chess, I mean."

She became even more convinced that for him, there was no clear distinction between business and pleasure. She narrowed her eyes. "You're too hard on yourself. Games are supposed to be fun, not life lessons."

"There's room for improvement in everything we do," he said. "Don't you think we should always try to be better?"

"No."

"You didn't even pause to think about that."

Lola looked at the tablecloth. "It's more important to me that I'm comfortable in my own skin. I'd rather look around and be happy with what I have than always wondering what's around the corner."

"You can do that and strive to be better."

That kind of thinking was for people who were in an elevator on the way up. She was fine on the ground floor, where her feet were stable. Someone like Beau had a long distance to fall. "My life may be simple, but I'm content," she said. "I have what I need."

"I don't believe you," Beau said. "Or maybe I don't want to believe you. I'm never content. And I'm happiest when I'm conquering myself."

"Spoken like a true king," she said, nodding up at his profile.

He shook his head, his eyes forward. "No. A king conquers others."

Chapter Nine

Lola ate everything put in front of her—oysters on the half shell, beef tenderloin, roasted vegetables, berry soufflé tart.

Beau looked as satisfied as she felt full. "Ready for our next stop?" he asked as she finished off her last bite.

She wiped her mouth with the napkin in her lap. She didn't answer—the question was rhetorical. Whether or not she was ready didn't matter.

Beau scooted his chair out and stood. His smile was inauthentic, but Lola doubted anyone else noticed. Except for Churchill, they seemed more interested in perfecting their own imitations at happiness. Lola was the only woman at the table who hadn't pulled out a compact at some point to check her lipstick. Maybe she should have, but she didn't own one. The men were the same with their cell phones. Beau hadn't so much as glanced at his phone once that she'd noticed, and that surprised her. A man like him had to be busy all times of the day.

"Thank you for such great company tonight," Beau told the table, "but you'll have to excuse us. Lola and I have pressing plans."

Glenn came around to shake Beau's hand. "Olivier, how come we've never had that meeting?"

"You're an important man, sir."

The mayor teased Beau by winking at Lola. "Let's get one on the books," he said to Beau. "Have your secretary call mine."

"Consider it done."

Glenn smiled and nodded over at Lola. "Word of advice? Don't screw this up. I like this one. She's good for you."

Lola thanked the mayor and let him hug her before they left.

Out front, Beau went to the valet stand while Lola waited at the curb.

"That went well with Churchill," he said, his hands in his pockets as he returned to her. "All I needed was a meeting. The rest will take care of itself."

"I don't know if anyone's ever told you, but you can be very convincing," Lola said.

"But these things aren't about business. They're about networking and relationships. Churchill liked you. That's the only reason he gave me the time of the day."

"I think that was a compliment," she said. "So thank you."

He turned all the way to her. "No, this is a compliment. You're not just beautiful, but smart too. Churchill saw that. I see it."

"You can drop the act," she said. "I don't think the valets need to hear it."

He took her chin and pulled her mouth an inch from his. "I have to be a certain person in my professional life. I try not to be that in my personal. I may not always be forthcoming or virtuous, but when it comes to you, I don't act." He kissed her softly without lingering. "Don't underestimate yourself. You may have just earned me a great deal of money."

Lola twisted her face away at the mention of money. "I'm so glad."

"You should be. Nothing puts me in a better mood than making money."

Lola stepped back a little. She couldn't fall under his spell. Once, she'd been unimpressed with Beau's past because attaining his level of success often meant screwing someone over.

"What's wrong?" he asked.

"This meeting I helped you get...it isn't anything illegal or corrupt, is it?"

"He's the mayor, Lola."

She pursed her lips. "And elected officials are always angels."

"You have nothing to worry about it. It's all legit."

"Well, what's it about?"

"You really want to know?"

Why did she care? Beau's business was just that— his business. It had nothing to do with her. She'd convinced herself coming into this that spending the night with Beau would be easiest if he were just a stranger. But to say she wasn't curious about him would've been lying to herself. She nodded. "Sure."

"The meeting's about tax breaks and incentives for angel investors—those of us putting a lot of money into early-stage startups. Los Angeles has access to so much talent with USC and UCLA, plus the arts and entertainment industry—we need to work on keeping that talent here. But it'll follow the money if it goes to a city with more benefits."

"Why wouldn't he want to do that?"

"It's not that he doesn't want to, he's just not very tech forward. I'm sure he has people telling him different things, but I want to lay it out for him from the perspective of someone who has a vested interest in this city. Unfortunately, he thinks my businessman's heart has bad intentions."

Lola lifted an eyebrow. "Does it?"

"Tax credits are good for me, no doubt. The more money I save, the more I can invest, and that's potential to earn. Local talent would also help me. If a startup is headquartered in Los Angeles or does significant business here, they're on my radar."

"How come?"

"Because it's good for our economy. Los Angeles is my home, and I want it to stay competitive with places like San Francisco and New York."

Lola could understand that—she'd never lived anywhere else, so she was particularly fond of L.A. Still, Beau would always be a man with a bottom line. "I can see why Churchill is skeptical," she said. "It's hard to believe you don't have an ulterior motive."

"I'll be upfront about how I benefit in the short

and long term. I just want Los Angeles to benefit equally."

It wasn't until a silver sports car pulled up that Lola remembered Warner. "What about the limo?"

"We're finished with that portion of the night," Beau said. "I'll be driving to our next destination."

"Your hotel," Lola said.

"Not yet."

The valet hopped out of the car, beaming. "This is why I love working these events. The Lamborghini's no joke, dude. I mean *sir*. That was my first time driving the Aventador Roadster."

"How was it?" Beau asked.

"Fucking awesome. I had to restrain myself from finding out the zero-to-sixty."

"It's about three seconds," Beau said.

The valet looked Lola up and down. "Lucky bastard."

Beau laughed as he took out his wallet. "I won't argue with that."

The boy's eyes bugged wide when he accepted his tip. "And I won't argue with that! Thank you, sir."

Beau waved him off to let Lola in the car himself. The three-quarter doors rose up like wings. Inside, only the dashboard lights glowed in the dark.

Once Beau was behind the wheel, Lola found the button on the console that lowered their windows. "It's such a nice night," she said.

"I'm not really a wind-in-my-hair type of guy," he protested.

"Can't you fake it for a night?"

He shook his head at her teasing smile. "I suppose one night won't kill me."

Before he pulled into the street, he reached over and undid Lola's hair with one hand.

"It'll get messy," she said when it fell around her shoulders.

He looked at her, winked and stepped on the gas. "It already is."

Soon, they were speeding down Sunset Boulevard. "Beau," Lola called over the engine. Her hands wrapped around her neck and hair. "We're going fast."

"What other way is there?" he asked, grinning ear to ear. "Relax. Enjoy the ride."

She forced her fingers to loosen. The road seemed to open just for them. Beau navigated swiftly through traffic, swerving between cars, racing yellow lights, leaving no room for error so her heart raced with them. Neon lights blurred together as they passed bars, souvenir shops, comedy clubs. Black palm trees silhouetted against the billboards. She released her hair, put her head back and closed her eyes.

"You're so beautiful, Lola," Beau said. "The most breathtaking thing."

It *was* beautiful. She'd never felt so unattached to everything, even her body. She opened her eyes. Nature and commercialism and Beau were all around her. She loved the car and the new way it allowed her to experience the boulevard she thought she'd seen from every angle.

But she shot up from the headrest when she noticed where they were. "Beau, you're not taking me to—"

"Hey Joe?" he interrupted. "No. Not even I'm that cruel."

They passed the bar and stopped several blocks down. She knew the building they parked in front of since she used to walk by it frequently on her way to see Johnny at Hey Joe. "What are we doing?" she asked as he rolled up the windows.

"A nightcap."

"Does it have to be here? Can't we do it at the hotel or something?"

"It has to be here." He got out of the car and then opened her door for her. He placed his large hand at the nape of her neck, guiding her down an alley until they were almost in a parking lot.

"What is this?" Lola asked. "I've never been here."

Beau knocked once on large side door. "Used to be a speakeasy."

The bouncer leaned out, then stepped aside to let them in.

"You must come here often," Lola said over her shoulder.

"I like their oysters."

"Is oyster a euphemism for something else?"

He laughed. "Would that bother you?"

"No." She looked forward again. "Euphemisms don't bother me at all."

They passed through a corridor. The fur articles in the coat check were almost too much for her—it was only the beginning of fall, and it was Los Angeles for heaven's sake. She parted heavy gold velvet curtains to enter a dimly lit room. To her right, a man in a suit clinked tulip glasses with a woman in pearls.

Despite being a few blocks from Hey Joe, Lola didn't worry about running into anyone she knew. These were Beau's people, not hers. She started to tell him she didn't like it but stopped. Underneath and behind the pretentiousness were gritty brick walls and aged-leather booths the color of whiskey. An impressive backlit wall of liquor glowed bronze. In the center of the room sat a grand piano, and the pianist played "Heart-Shaped Box."

"By the look on your face, I guess you're a Nirvana fan," Beau said.

"I don't think I could've dreamed up a stranger song for this place."

Beau ordered from the bartender while she watched the pianist play.

"The first time I heard Nirvana was on the radio the day Kurt Cobain died," she said.

"I remember that day," Beau said. "I was a teenager, so you must've been..."

"Pretty young. I fell in love, though. Johnny hates grunge. He's rock 'n' roll straight through." She took the drink Beau offered her without looking away. "How about you?"

"I'm with Johnny on this one."

"Really?" She glanced at him.

"Don't look so surprised. Pink Floyd got me through a lot of late nights at the office."

Lola stopped bobbing her head and took a sip of her drink. She looked down into the glass.

"Do you like it?" Beau asked. "It's bourbon."

"Bourbon isn't really my thing, but this isn't bad." She drank a little more. "It's smooth. Sweet."

"Fruity." He smelled his glass. "Pappy Van Winkle, barrel-aged twenty-three years. Rare, partly because it takes so long to age and there just isn't enough. Take your time—something like this should be savored."

"In other words, it's expensive."

"It depends on what you mean by expensive. Money is not the same thing as worth, and drinking a glass of this with you is worth a lot to me."

Lola made a noise of appreciation, and not just for the drink. The sweet alcohol burn, the leathery smell of the bar, the dim lights, Beau's deep voice—it was a heady combination.

"How do you feel?" he asked.

"Relaxed."

He smiled. "Me too."

"You, relaxed? I bet that's as rare as this drink." The two martinis she'd had at the gala had done nothing for her, but drinking this bourbon was like falling into a warm embrace.

"That would be a safe bet," he said.

"How much do you work? Be honest."

"Right now, I work a lot. Back when I was trying to create something from nothing, though, I barely stopped to eat."

"Your family was okay with that?"

"I did it for them as much as for myself."

"What about your friends? Girlfriends?"

Beau raised an eyebrow. "I'm something of a loner

if you haven't noticed."

"Even now?"

He hesitated. "A man with money trusts his enemies more than his friends."

She tried to picture her life without Johnny and Vero and the people she saw at the bar almost nightly. While she was there, Beau was at events with eager reporters in his face and people who were often trying to get something from him. She put her hand on his arm. "That must be hard."

Beau took a moment to respond. "When you're nice to me, it makes me want to kiss you," he warned.

"What about when I'm mean?" She allowed herself a playful smile.

He palmed her lower back and drew her close to his side. "It makes me want to be mean back." He slid his hand over the curve of her backside but stopped.

"Your patience is admirable," she said, hoping he didn't notice her slight gasp between words.

"My patience is thin."

"You're the one carting me from place to place."

His eyes gleamed. "You're ready for the hotel?"

Her gaze dropped to his lips, his bowtie and jumped back up. He curled his fingers into her dress.

"I'll take your inability to answer as a yes," he said.

He took her hand and walked her out of the lounge. Coming out of the alley, she turned left, but he pulled her back. "This way."

"But the car—"

"This wasn't our stop," he said, leading her in the opposite direction. "I'd just heard about a shipment of that bourbon and I wanted you to try it."

"Then where are we going?"

He dropped her hand and didn't answer. Her heart began to pound as they walked west. He glanced over at her with that impatient look he'd gotten right before he'd kissed her on the red carpet.

"Here?" she asked when he stopped walking. "Is this supposed to be funny?"

"What's funny?" he asked, his eyebrows lowering.

"I'm not going in there. I can't."

"You can," he said, "and you will."

She looked behind Beau. On the brick wall a pink neon sign flashed the word *Girls* at her over and over. She dried her palms on her dress. After spending an evening with Los Angeles's elite, Cat Shoppe seemed like a cruel joke.

It wasn't. Any teasing, gleaming or admiration in Beau's eyes was gone. "You aren't too good for a strip club?"

They must've looked that way on the outside—she made up in a gown, he strangled by his bowtie.

She was far from too good for it. She'd once been a part of it. A lifetime ago, Lola had spent her nights dancing at Cat Shoppe, getting caught up in the money and the partying and forming bonds with girls she no longer spoke to. When people found out she'd been a stripper, they always wanted to know why.

"Why are you doing this?" her mom asked from across the Formica table. Pleaded.

"For the money." Lola's tone was dry. "Isn't that what it's all about?"

Dina shook her head. "You're only eighteen. This isn't how I raised you."

Lola smiled thinly. "You think because I lived under your roof, you raised me? Come on, Mom. I raised myself. Nobody ever looked out for me but me."

Dina suddenly and visibly shook with anger. "How can you say that? I worked here day after day to put food in your mouth." She slammed both fists on the tabletop. "I did that for you! I sacrificed my life for a child I didn't even want."

Lola barely flinched. That Dina hadn't wanted her was no secret. "Think what you like," Lola said, standing. "I'm not quitting."

"Then don't come back home when it blows up in your face. I won't watch you do this to yourself."

Lola left without looking back.

She'd said she'd done it for money, but it'd been more than that. Lola had not only loved to dance, she'd loved how it'd made her feel, how men had looked at her, how the money had put her in charge of her life. It gave her control, especially over men, something her dad had taken from her by walking out one morning and never coming home.

Beau watched her intently. She wasn't willing to share that part of her life with him, and she wouldn't give him the satisfaction of a reaction. She walked right by him, by the bouncer and into the club.

The music hit Lola before anything. On the main stage of the dark club was a half-naked woman who looked in her early forties. On her palms and knees, she snaked toward an outstretched, dollar-waving hand.

Across the room, Beau talked to a bartender. Even

though it'd been eight years since she'd left, Lola turned away in case anyone she knew still worked there.

A few moments later, Beau closed in on her back. "It's not top-dollar bourbon," he said, reaching around to hold the glass in front of her, "but it'll do."

She stared at the drink but didn't take it.

"What do you think of her?" he asked about the woman on the main stage. "Personally, she's not my type. She wouldn't get any of my dollars. Not like you."

Lola turned her head from the woman. "It doesn't do anything for me," Lola said. "I think we should go."

Beau took her chin with his other hand and forced her to look back at the stage. "We're not going anywhere. Does this make you hot?"

She wrestled her face away. "No."

"It will," he said. "Come with me."

Chapter Ten

Lights lasered through the dark strip club in every direction. Women danced on small podiums set apart from the main stage. The music was loud, but Lola wished it were deafening so she wouldn't have to hear her thoughts. She'd gone from a prize on Beau's arm to trailing behind him with her head down to hide her face.

She'd danced for men like Beau before, men who liked to flaunt that they had money to burn. She'd been most careful around that type. When she danced, music lived in her. It was intoxicating. Men could tell, and it was dangerous for them to believe they had that kind of effect on a woman.

Beau led her down a hallway of doors. If one was open, the lights were on, and it was chipped-paint black inside with just a pole and some scattered chairs.

He stopped at the last room. "Here we are, my queen."

"Why are we here?" She controlled the impulse to

fidget by crossing her arms.

Beau gestured inside. "Go on. I warned you not everything would be comfortable."

It was the VIP room. The round stage, centered in a round room, ensured a view from every angle. One pole cut through the middle. Red velvet walls bled into Bordeaux-colored sofas that lined the space. The bass of the music from the main stage thumped through the room.

Lola looked over her shoulder. A woman in only a shiny gold thong and pasties over her nipples came in. Numerous metallic ribbons threaded her hair. She trailed a finger down Beau's shoulder. "Good evening, sir," she said. "I'm Golden."

"And I'm Angel." Another woman stepped into the room. Her fur-lined, white baby-doll negligee matched her G-string. She placed a headband with red horns over her blonde hair. "Or Devil," she said pleasantly. "Your choice." Lola didn't recognize either of them.

Beau crossed the room and fell into a sofa. He tugged on his collar a little. Golden pushed some buttons on a keypad and the room changed to fiery pink as the music started. A spotlight shone over the stage.

Angel danced first. Beau watched her spin around the pole, her negligee billowing to reveal a flat stomach. She landed with ease on towering heels and smiled at him. He remained impassive.

The lights changed from pink to deep purple. Golden sat next to Beau and whispered in his ear. He nodded. Lola stood motionless while Golden straddled

Beau, hovering her lips above his as she danced for him. The room was blue now, turning the red velvet a blood-black color. Beau looked past Golden to Angel when she bent, touched her toes and displayed her barely-there underwear for him. His eyes shifted to Lola. "Join me."

She shook her head. Watching him with another woman did nothing for her except spark some disappointment. It hadn't occurred to her that he might involve anyone else in their evening.

"It's not a request," he said.

Lola went to sit by him. Golden's breasts nearly touched his cheek with each movement.

"Are you enjoying this?" he asked.

"Why would you pay for an evening with me just to watch them?"

"I'm still with you." He leaned over and kissed her harder than he had earlier. When she jerked back, he reached up to keep her there. His lips and hand were warm. Pulling away had been instinct, but they'd be doing far more soon. Her jaw and shoulders relaxed. For now, it was just a kiss.

"It's sweet," he whispered into her mouth, "the taste of your submission." He pecked her again and looked up. "Touch her."

Lola had momentarily forgotten about the other women. Golden's fingers were soft as she combed Lola's hair away from her face.

"Have you ever been with a woman?" Beau asked.

"Once. To try."

"Did you enjoy it?"

159

"Not enough to do it again."

Golden ran a knuckle down Lola's cheek. She traced her way down the strap of Lola's dress to the neckline, but Beau grabbed her wrist. "Wait."

She dropped her arm to her side. Angel worked the pole, sliding over it as if it were silk against her skin, possessing it with her legs and hands. The white fabric of her top shone under the spotlight as she peeled it off. She stopped there. The topless-only rule hadn't changed since Lola's time there.

"Kiss," Beau said.

Lola snapped her head back to Beau. He was watching her, not Angel. The room became hotter. He nodded once. Golden leaned over and put her mouth to Lola's. Gently, she ran her tongue along Lola's bottom lip.

Lola backed away a little. Beau had left the taste of liquor in her mouth. The woman's cherry lip balm would replace it. Any other night she might've preferred the cherry, but tonight she wanted Beau's bitter flavor. Golden chased her down for another kiss as she felt Lola's breast through her dress. Lola shut her eyes briefly and gave into the shameful desire that it was actually Beau touching her.

"Beau," Lola moaned, not because she enjoyed it, but because she didn't.

"Tell me what you want, sweetheart," he said.

Golden tweaked Lola's nipples into hardening.

"If you don't like it," he said, "just say so."

"I don't like it."

"Enough," Beau said. Golden pulled away,

obviously confused.

"Now you, Lola," he said when the song changed. He signaled Angel to get down.

"But—"

"It's not up for discussion."

"Ask them to leave," Lola said. "If I dance, it's only for you."

Beau's lids lowered a little, but he blinked suddenly and the lusty look was gone. "How many times do I need to ask before you do what I say? Hmm? You challenge me at every turn. Get up on the stage and dance."

She stood.

"Now tell me why you're doing this," he said.

She opened her mouth, breathed softly. With the hardness in his voice, her determination not to enjoy herself slipped. He already had all the power, but he wanted more. With each passing hour, he pushed the limits of her submission. Not even Johnny held that kind of complete control over her.

"Why?" he repeated.

"Because you told me to."

"Very good."

She climbed onto the platform. The spotlight and room had turned red.

"You get paid either way," Beau said. "So try to enjoy it."

With one hand around the pole, Lola circled the stage. The gown would inhibit her, but she got the feeling Beau wouldn't mind. The music was fast. She found a slower beat within it. She jumped, grabbed on and spun with one leg partially hooked around the pole. Angel and Golden sat on both sides of Beau. He was unblinking, unwavering in his attention. Even in the red haze, she saw the gleam in his eyes, the black shape of his bowtie. Her body rattled like a speaker with the music's bass.

Facing Beau, she raised her arms behind her. She snaked down the metal, cool through the back of her dress, and back up. Beau stood suddenly and walked to the base of the stage. He took her calf and pressed his lips to the inside of her knee. His mouth left wet spots on her dress as he kissed up her thigh to her hip. He gripped her, nuzzling the fabric between her legs.

Lola's breaths swelled from her stomach. She felt him—felt him *there*—acutely for the first time. God, it was unfair. He'd barely touched her and her will to fight him dissolved in seconds. She put one hand in his hair and pulled it with all the betrayal, shame and arousal she felt.

He looked up at her.

"Touching's not permitted in here," she said.

His smile was more than just crooked and sexy. For all her effort to hide, that smile told her he knew he had her. He turned and cleared both women from the room with a word.

He backed away to the sofa, and this time, Lola went to him. She pulled her dress up around her thighs. One knee went outside his hip and one stayed between his legs. She held on to the cushion behind his head. She was careful not to touch him as she danced over his lap, but now and then her skin would brush against the fabric of his tuxedo pants. When he looked as though he might touch her, she got up, pushed his knees apart. She let her hands wander over her body as she swayed her hips. She dipped a hand between her legs and slid the other up her neck.

Beau reached for her, but she stepped back and shook her head. "You can't—"

"Come back here." His level tone left no room for play. "Don't deny me when I'm like this."

When she was back at his knees, he took her wrist in one hand. "Kneel."

She got on the floor.

"You're all red," he said.

"It's the lighting."

"No, it isn't. You're hot." He let go of her and pressed his cold tumbler to the side of her neck. She sucked in a breath with the chill. Condensation trickled between her breasts. He lifted the glass to her lips. She tilted her head back and let the liquor run down her throat.

He set the drink aside and nodded at his lap. "Take it out," he said quietly.

This was it. This was why she was here. She had wondered several times what exactly lay under his suit, what was the source of his unshakeable confidence— now she would know for sure. Hold it in her hand.

Her fingers were slow and shaky as she undid his fly. He lifted his hips for her to pull his pants down. Through his underwear, she pressed her palm against the bulging outline of him. His head fell back. She lifted the ends of his dress shirt, dragging her fingertips up the hard crevices of his stomach. His body expanded with each breath.

"Don't tease me, Lola," he said. "I want your red lips on me."

There was new desperation in his voice that made Lola ache badly for him. And this deal—this promise—she'd already made it. Johnny, even, had made it. So she put a bullet through her guilt and gave Beau what he wanted.

She pulled him out, looking into his eyes while she took him in her mouth. He fisted her hair, then stroked it, then pulled it again. He thrust up, hitting the back of her throat. She tried to taste even more, wanting him deeper, wanting him to the last inch, but still he was too much, every bit as big and daunting as she'd suspected.

"Your mouth alone could ruin me." She paused, unsure how he'd meant that, but he kept her going with a hand on her head. "Don't stop," he said. "I want to be ruined."

With her tongue, she traced him—the ridge of his head, the veins of his thick shaft.

"You're driving me to the edge," he said. "I don't know whether to come, or bend you over and finally take you."

She became ravenous from his rumbling, suggestive words. He responded, pushing her down so he was crammed to her throat with every bob of her head. Her underwear dampened with the way he thoroughly fucked her mouth. With both his hands tight in her hair, he came. She gripped the red velvet cushion and swallowed everything.

There was calm in the eye of the chaos, in the labored breaths, the pounding music, the room, which had turned pink again sometime during it all. But while they looked at each other, anything else, including the regret she thought she should feel, faded into the background.

On impulse, Lola stretched up and kissed him on the mouth. He wouldn't lower his head to meet her or move his arms from his sides. She pressed her hands down on his thighs, her breasts into his wall of a chest. His body breathed beneath her.

"How'd you know?" she asked. "How did you know I'd react like this?"

He seemed to stiffen under her. "It's not even midnight," he said. "We aren't finished."

"I know."

He touched her cheek with his whole palm. "You're burning up."

She bit her lip. She could feel it too. "It's a good thing."

He helped her to her feet, and they left the room while it was blue.

"You're supposed to tip them," Lola remembered once they were outside again.

"It's taken care of. They won't be millionaires after this, but they've been well compensated."

"Millionaire," she repeated to herself. She still couldn't wrap her head around it, and it'd be a while before she could. After tonight, she'd be a millionaire and all this would be over. The thought didn't give her as much comfort as it once had.

◆ ◆ ◆

In the car, driving down Sunset at a much easier speed, Beau asked Lola what she planned to do with the money.

"You already know," she answered. "We're buying Hey Joe."

"I know what *he* wants. But what about you? You're the one doing all the work."

Lola balked. "It makes me feel cheap when you say that."

"Believe me, sweetheart. You aren't cheap."

She shook her head and sighed up at the Lamborghini's roof. "I want us to be happy and have a shot at a real future."

"But what do you want for yourself?"

"That's what I want. Making Johnny happy makes me happy."

"Fine. Everybody's happy. Now give me something real. A new car? A trip to New York City? What're you going to do for yourself?"

"To tell you the truth, I haven't given it much thought. I'm okay with what I've got."

"Slinging drinks is what you want to do forever? Haven't you ever asked yourself what you'd do if money weren't an issue? You have some freedom now."

"Not until the sun comes up," Lola said.

Beau scoffed. "I'm glad to see one blowjob hasn't killed your spirit."

What a blowjob it'd been. Lola was incredibly turned on, and she'd barely even been touched. She made an effort to control herself, even though she squirmed in her seat a little. "What do you want me to say? That I love to paint landscapes, or I've always dreamed of backpacking through Europe? I don't and I haven't. Not everyone has hobbies or dreams. That's not the kind of life I live."

Beau slammed on the brakes. The car behind them swerved and honked. "So tell me what kind of life you live."

"What are you doing?" Lola asked. "You can't just stop in the middle of the road."

"Conventional methods aren't working," he said. "I don't want platitudes. Just give me a real answer."

"Are you drunk?" Lola asked. "You're drunk, aren't you?"

"I didn't even finish my drink. I want to know more about the girl I played darts with. Who you are when he's not around."

Lola shook her head. "You're getting sentimental on me just because I let you come in my mouth?"

Beau barked a laugh. "Can you blame me? You're so charming."

She smiled through the honking of passing cars. "You're really going to stay here?"

He nodded. "Here's an easier question. Tell me something you *don't* want out of life."

She squinted through the windshield. It was an easier question, and even though she'd never articulated it, the answer didn't come with difficultly. "I don't want Johnny to lose his sense of self-worth along with the bar. I was afraid if he didn't have Hey Joe, he'd have to

167

start over somewhere else, and he'd feel like he'd failed."

"Failure's good for us, you know."

She looked over at him. "Are you saying I shouldn't have taken the deal?"

"I'm saying you can't be the sacrifice for the fulfillment of his dreams." He took his foot off the brake and resumed driving. "When he asked what you wanted to do with the money, what'd you say?"

Lola chewed the inside of her cheek. She wasn't sure Johnny *had* asked. There'd never been any other option. She was using the money to keep them intact. Johnny knew the ins and outs of Hey Joe. He was master of that domain. Maybe it wasn't her dream job, but she'd never had a dream job—so she wasn't losing anything. Only, Beau seemed to think there was more to it, and now she wondered if there was. "You've made your point."

"You need to figure out what you want," he said. "Not what you want *for him.* Then you need to tell him."

"I don't know if you're right," she said, "but you might not be wrong."

He pulsed his eyebrows at her once. "That's a start. So what would it take to get you to figure it out?"

They happened to be in a familiar part of town. Giving in to Beau had loosened her up a bit, and he was working hard to shine his spotlight on her, so she decided to help him out by moving under it a little more. "How about a trip down memory lane?"

"What'd you have in mind?" he asked right away.

She pointed in front of them. "Take a right up

here." After only a few minutes of driving, she told him to park at a curb. "See that place?" she asked, nodding through the window.

"The Lucky Egg," Beau read the flickering sign off the corner diner.

"When I was a kid, my mom worked there. Days *and* nights. The life of a single mom."

"Where was your dad?"

"Gone. I don't have a lot of memories of him. I remember weird things, though, like the smell of his shampoo when he'd pick me up before leaving for work, or the time he kissed my elbow after I'd fallen climbing a tree in the backyard. Then it was just me and her."

"Have you seen him since?"

"No. If he'd come back, I think my mom would've killed him. She got so angry after he left. It flipped a switch in her. They married right out of high school, so she'd never been on her own. She thought we were going to lose the house, or they were going to take our car. She'd get really rundown from working so much."

"Sounds the opposite of my mom. When my dad died, she became helpless. I kept waiting for that maternal survival instinct to kick in, but it didn't."

"I don't even think it was maternal instinct for my mom. She just saw me as this little person who drained her meager bank account. Around seventeen, I moved in with some older kids. We partied a lot. The first night I went to Hey Joe, Johnny should've kicked me out because I was underage. Guess he took pity on me, though. He gave me a tequila shot instead."

"Or he was trying to get in your pants."

Lola shook her head. "We didn't start sleeping together for a while, actually. And when we did, I didn't take it seriously until he broke up with me."

"I see. Obviously that didn't last."

Lola kept her eyes out the window. "He was sick of me screwing around. He gave me an ultimatum—grow up or get out. Quit the drugs, the partying, the—" She paused. "He saved me. Turned my life around. If not for him, I don't know where I'd be."

"You should give yourself more credit. You're a fighter. That much is obvious."

She finally looked at Beau. "If you're fighting against the wrong thing, the only person you'll hurt is yourself." The digital clock on the dashboard changed. "I'm sure this isn't how you want to spend your precious few hours," she added.

He looked at the clock too, then out the windshield. He turned the car around. "What happened to your mom?" he asked.

"Oh, she still works there." Lola turned her face away when he peered at her.

They didn't speak again until they were on Santa Monica Boulevard. "How many women have you done this with?" Lola asked.

"None."

"You expect me to believe that?"

"Why would I lie?"

"To seem like less of an asshole."

Beau chuckled. "What does it matter if you think I'm an asshole? I already got you here. If you don't like me by the time we're done, it's all the same to me."

Her eyes drifted to the clock again. She assumed they were now going to the hotel, but she didn't ask. Beau had his own agenda. "If you don't care either way, then I could be anyone."

"That's not true at all." He sighed and shifted in his seat. "I've met a lot of women over the years. All kinds—blonde, brunette, athletic, short, sweet, married, single. Something's different about you, Lola."

Lola didn't think of herself as the same as or different from anyone. But she could guess the things she was compared to Beau's usual women. For one, she didn't go for bullshit, but his world turned for it.

"Something's different about you too," she admitted. Lola wasn't proud that she'd pegged Beau as another corporate asshole during their first meeting on the sidewalk. He'd proved her wrong during their darts game, but that'd only lasted until his proposition. Then he'd been worse than an asshole in her eyes. She worried he was proving her wrong again. That would make the evening entirely different. The Beau she'd agreed to spend the night with was the repugnant one who'd offered money for her body—not the sexy one she'd known before that.

"It's always been my opinion that different is good," he said. "I hope you agree."

"You know, you aren't the first man to try and sleep with me behind Johnny's back."

"Did you?" Beau asked.

"Did I what?"

"Sleep with them."

"No," Lola said emphatically.

"Good." He hit his blinker and slowed for a light. "I don't like cheating. It's for people who don't think they can win. If you don't believe in yourself enough to play by the rules, you aren't worthy of the prize."

"Are we still talking about sex?"

"Cheating is always weak, no matter the circumstances."

"Beau, some people—lots of people—might call *this* cheating."

"I don't. And I didn't try to sleep with you behind his back like you said. It all happened in front of his face. Johnny's aware of everything. He had his chance to put a stop to it."

"Have you ever turned down a million dollars?" Lola asked wryly. Beau had been desperate before. Had he already forgotten how that felt?

"Sure I have," he said. "When the company on the table was worth more."

"I'm not talking about business, Beau. We're people. I'm talking about lives."

He didn't speak. Money, sex, worth, people—it all shaded into a gray area for them. Had anyone asked her before all this, she would've answered that a dollar amount couldn't be put on a person's life. She still believed that, but the concepts were no longer completely unrelated in her mind.

"Let's not argue about it," Beau said, sighing again. Ahead, they were entering Beverly Hills. "I don't want you wasting any more energy. You're going to need it soon."

Chapter Eleven

On the sixteenth floor of the Four Seasons Los Angeles at Beverly Hills, Beau and Lola exited a gold elevator. They'd been quiet since the car. To their left, a large window showcased the dark sky and the faint silhouette of mountains on the horizon. She followed him the opposite direction past the elevator bank to a hallway. At the end of it was a single black-lacquer door with a knob in the center. The corridor was long and carpeted, muting their steps. As they approached the door, her heart beat faster. It'd been nine years since she'd been with a man other than Johnny. And about that long since she'd wanted to.

When they reached the door, Beau pulled out his key and unlocked it with a _click_.

Lola's stomach was beyond butterflies—she was sure an entire zoo had been released inside her. She stared at the doorway, which was a threshold, a point of no return, a choice plain and simple. Sweat beaded on her upper lip.

"It's too late to turn back now," Beau said.

She didn't look away. "Not if I give back the money."

Beau let the door close. "I know what you're doing." He walked to her, his steps deliberate. "If I force you into that room, then it isn't your choice."

"Nobody forced me here," she said. "I made every decision. I had to. That doesn't make my choices right."

"Lola," he said softly. "You don't have to put on a show. Tonight is about you and me only. Take control of what you want."

She glanced up at him. "You think you know what I want?"

He moved forward until the wall was at her back. He pushed a hand in the neckline of her dress. "You're right," he said. "I have no idea what you want. Since your nipple isn't hard between my fingers. And you weren't wet earlier as you sucked me off."

"Just because you manipulate my body's reaction," her voice wavered, "doesn't mean I want this. You can't control my mind or my heart no matter what you say."

His hand stilled. The muscles in his jaw flexed. "You're so fucking concerned about your heart? Keep it. I'll use your body. I won't be gentle. And when I'm finished, you can have it back."

He could take what he wanted. It wouldn't mean anything to her. It shouldn't. But his words were even more erotic than his touch. Her legs trembled from them, threatening to give out.

Lola tried to push him off, but he grabbed her

wrist with his free hand and pinned it above her head. "This is what you want, isn't it?" he asked. "For me to take your choice away? Then no one will have to know that you want this just as badly as I do. That you wanted it the night we met."

She shook her head rapidly. His nearness smothered whatever sense she had left. She was becoming the puddle of desire she'd been at the strip club.

"Let me help you out," he said when she didn't speak. "You say, 'Yes, Beau.' Then I open the hotel room door. And every time I tell you what to do, you say…"

She fixated on his bowtie, breathing hard.

"I'm sorry, I didn't catch that. Can you speak up?" he asked.

She looked up at the sharpness of his tone. "Yes. Yes, Beau."

"Good." He released her and backed away. He opened the door again. The ghost of his grip pulsed around her wrist. "Ask yourself this," he said. "Do you have to want this to do it? Or are you going to do it anyway?"

She looked between him and the door. She was going to do it anyway. The decision shed a layer of resistance she'd been hiding behind. She entered the suite, where the only light came from the distant cityscape.

"Wait here until I call for you," Beau said.

She didn't move. Her nerves melted away. She was in Beau's hands now and if the past few hours were any indication, it would be an experience she'd never forget.

Glass clinked. The faucet ran. After minutes had passed, Beau spoke from somewhere in the suite. "Come to the bedroom."

"I don't know which way," she said. Directly in front of her was a piano and windowed door that led out to the balcony.

"You'll find me," he said. "And you'll do it on your hands and knees."

Her dry throat protested when she swallowed.

That a tyrant in everything else would also be a tyrant in the bedroom didn't surprise her—that there would be a show of strength, a struggle of wills, an expected submission—she might have guessed. But knowing and doing were two different things. She'd never lived it. She knew girls from the club who had. Some liked it, some didn't. For most, it wasn't that simple.

Lola sank to her hands and knees faster than she would've thought. The tile was hard underneath her, but she was on the carpet soon. The dress caught between her legs while she crawled, slowing her down. Beau didn't rush her. She went the opposite direction of a flat screen TV, past a round dining table with several chairs. As she got closer, warmer, her breath came faster and her legs seemed heavier—the tender place between them, specifically.

She found Beau on the edge of the bed, still fully dressed except for his jacket.

"Don't stop now," he said. "You're almost here."

She didn't remember ever crawling one day of her

adult life. Inside she screamed at herself to get off the floor, but she closed her eyes, inhaled and quieted it. This wasn't about her.

Or was it? Beau had unusual power over her. She'd never been put in this position while someone else watched, nor did she think she'd allow it from anyone else, even with the money. She was still dressed, but she felt stripped and exposed. Crawling for him was a form of intimacy. She opened her eyes.

"Your struggle is a thing to watch," Beau said just loud enough for her to hear. "If I thought you'd respond honestly, I'd ask you how it feels to submit."

"It hurts my knees."

A corner of his mouth lifted. "Maybe you can give me something less tactile."

"I feel…helpless." Vulnerability was rare for her. She'd learned young that it didn't pay to be vulnerable. But with her helplessness came a relief that left her confused. She had no responsibility other than giving Beau what he asked for. No other choice. And it wasn't a bad thing. "That's what you want, isn't it?" she asked. "Me, helpless?"

"Don't tell me what you think I want to hear. You can tell me if you hate being on your hands and knees. Maybe I'll let you stand."

She stared at him, unmoving. He was going to make her say that she liked this out loud or he would take it away. She should've been thankful, but letting her stand felt like a punishment.

"Lola," he said. "Everything between us lives and dies in this room. It's safe."

Her fingers curled into the carpet, but not with frustration. The slow throb between her legs was stronger. Could Beau see it? Smell it? He looked as if he knew. "I don't."

"Don't what?"

"Hate it." She couldn't say much more without giving herself away. However gone she was, there was still a shred of Johnny in her she couldn't bring herself to betray. "You make it not repulsive."

"Well, not repulsive is something." There was such approval in his smile that she flushed. "But it'll be hard to do anything to you when you're so far away."

She finished crossing the room until she was at his feet.

He removed one cufflink, set it on the nightstand, then the other. Lola's heart beat between her breasts. Beau rolled up one sleeve, stood and leaned over her. He gathered up her dress and pulled it over her hips. He hiked up the panties he'd bought her, wedging them between her ass cheeks. His firm hand ran soothingly over her backside as if she were a treasured plaything. She bit her lip to keep any sounds inside.

"I'm going to take you apart," he said. "Find out what makes you feel so good it almost kills you."

"Don't."

He stroked her skin until he brushed a spot that made her jolt. He made a deep, rumbling noise from his chest. "Then I'll bring you back to life. Put you back together."

"Don't do it like this," she said. "Just use me and throw me out. I'm begging you."

"Let's see how deep your protest goes." He slid a fingertip under the elastic of her panties. "Mmm. Just as I suspected."

"What?" she breathed.

"You waxed. There's a chink in her armor."

"I didn't do it for you."

"Of course not." His hand grazed down one thigh to the top of her stocking and up again. "And your legs are shaved. I suppose that's not for me either."

She began to tremble lightly, alive with him so close to giving her what she'd been needing since the strip club—or longer. He circled her with two fingers and eased them in.

Her head bowed to meet the floor. She gasped when he went deeper. He murmured her name, moving in and out. Searching. At least the tile would've been cool against her face.

"Look at me."

She lifted her head.

"Make yourself wet," he said as he removed his hand and put two fingers to her lips. She opened, sucking him into her mouth and tasting herself on someone else's fingers for the first time.

He replaced them between her legs and leaned in to kiss her while rubbing her slippery clit from behind. When she convulsed and moaned, he took his hand away.

"Why are you stopping?" she demanded through the ringing in her ears.

"There's someone at the door. Would you mind?"

"What?" she asked.

"Answer the door."

She got up from her aching knees and wrists. Her dress fell around her legs. The heat in her chest and face pulsed with every punch of her heart.

It was room service. A young man wheeled a food cart into the living room, glancing at Lola from the corner of his eye. He positioned the cart and waited.

"One minute," she said.

She went to the bedroom. Beau was standing in the same spot, one sleeve rolled up and his hand splayed. "Yes?" he asked.

"It's room service. He brought food."

"And?"

"And...he needs his tip."

"So give it to him."

"You took my purse." She crossed her arms. "I have no money."

"Ah." He smiled and pulled his wallet from his pants. "Have him bring it in here."

"Bring it in here," she called without uncrossing her arms or looking away from Beau.

Beau blew out a laugh, shaking his head. "I suppose I could've done that."

When the cart was where Beau wanted it, the attendant took his tip, ducked his head and left.

Beau picked up a bowl. Before he could ask, she went to him. "Strawberries," she said. "Not very original."

"I'm not very original."

She picked one out of the bowl. He caught her wrist on the way to her mouth. She raised her eyes to him.

"Aren't you going to share?" he asked.

She lifted it to him. His teeth bit down just before her fingertips. He had a sexy mouth made for eating strawberries—and other things. She also took a bite and dropped the stem in the bowl. They had two more this way—him holding her, feeding him, feeding her.

He let go of her arm to pour them each some champagne.

"We're around the halfway point," Lola said, her mouth fizzing as she took a sip. "You're running out of time."

"We'll get to that." He took the champagne glass from her and set it down. "Hold your hands behind you."

She laced her fingers at the small of her back, jutting her breasts forward. Beau scooped whipped cream from the bowl with two fingers. He touched them to her closed lips. "How's it taste?"

She tested it with her tongue. "Light. Sweet."

"Have more," he suggested throatily.

She closed her mouth around his fingers and sucked him clean. "It's good," she said. There was grit in both their voices. "You should try it."

"I think I will." He smeared some whipped cream on the skin above her neckline. He took his time cleaning it off with his tongue, no matter how fast her breasts rose and fell.

He slipped one strap off her shoulder. "Keep your hands there," he said when she moved. He released the dress to her waist, trapping her arms with the straps. He took both breasts in his hands through her corset. She gasped up at the ceiling when he squeezed them.

"You like it a little rough," he said.

"I don't know."

"You'll know after tonight."

She swallowed, still looking up. "You said you wouldn't hurt me."

"I'll fuck you within an inch of your life, but it won't hurt. It will calm you. Your only job is to do what I say. And, of course, enjoy yourself."

He still had her breasts in a firm grip. It wasn't enough without his skin on hers, and she arched into his hands. "What if I don't like it rough?"

He let go. "Tell me now. I can do it in a way that you think we're making love."

Her face fell. "I don't want to make love."

"How does Johnny do it?"

For a second, she thought she'd misheard him. "I'm not talking to you about—"

"Don't protect him," Beau said. "He didn't protect you."

Her heart panged sharply. With her body in Beau's control and her mind out of focus, she was in no shape to dig in to that statement. "He's never been anything but Johnny with me," she said. "It's nice."

"Then I don't want to be nice." He pinched her nipple unexpectedly, and she inhaled sharply. He massaged it. "But I won't be mean, either."

"Thank you," she said.

He trussed one breast up and bent his head. "You are welcome, *ma chatte*." He sucked her nipple into his mouth, soaking the fabric around it.

"What does that mean?" she asked breathlessly.

He tugged her nipple between his teeth, and the pinch traveled down her body, ending between her legs. She released her hands when he yanked the dress over her hips. It puddled at her feet.

"It means," he said, and touched her boldly through her lace underwear, "this is mine."

"Only for a few more hours." As the inevitable loomed, her arousal was finally overtaking her determination not to give in. "Tick tock."

He raised an eyebrow at her. "Brave girl. Touch yourself with me." She reached into her underwear. He closed his warm hand around hers, guiding it along her.

He put his other hand to the front of his pants, massaging himself. "Tomorrow," he said, "you'll be home, and you'll think of this. How I feel against you. How we feel together."

She raised her chin. "Maybe."

His eyebrows rose even higher. "Maybe?"

"So far you haven't given me much to think about. Frankly, I'm not sure you have the guts."

"Excuse me?"

"You talk and talk, but here I am. You've barely touched me."

One corner of his mouth lifted. It was somehow both menacing and suggestive, and it dried her throat. He grabbed her shoulders in a flash, spun her to face the bed and pulled her back to his front. "Feel that, pussycat?" he asked, thrusting his erection into her lower back. He pushed her and she caught herself on the mattress. "Bend over," he said. "Put your arms out to your sides."

With her cheek against the bed, she stretched out and took two fistfuls of comforter. Her shoes propped her ass in the air at an uncomfortable angle, so she moved to take them off.

"Leave them," he said. "Lines you right up for my cock."

Her fists tightened. She wanted to turn around and watch him undress. Was his suit the source of his power? In her imagination, it wasn't—he was just as commanding with nothing between them except his hard-on.

He stripped her underwear down to her ankles. "You have no idea how hot you are in your black stockings." His zipper hissed. "Tell me you want it, Lola."

"I can't."

"Why not?"

"It's one thing to do it. It's another to want it."

"You'd walk away right now if I let you?"

She squeezed her eyes closed. She couldn't picture Johnny no matter how hard she tried, through the haze, through her heartbeat pounding in her brain. Beau's skin was warm against the backs of her thighs. He nudged himself between her legs.

"Answer me," he said. "Your secret stays here."

She was unraveling on the inside. Her nerves were surfacing—exposed and sensitive. Her mouth and her pussy were already slick. "I want it," she whispered.

"What do you want?"

"You. I want to feel you inside me."

He slid his crown up and down her slit. "Stay very still." He worked his way in, slow with every inch. It made him feel impossibly big. The comforter sucked into her open mouth when she gasped. She bit down on it. He placed his hands on the bed around her and his mouth at her ear. "You're so fucking beautiful in this position," he said. His chest pinned her down. "No escape, feeling every single movement between us." His voice vibrated against her back. He was still sinking himself in with extraordinary patience. He kissed her cheek and the corner of her mouth. "I want to hear you."

She moaned when she said, "Yes, Beau."

"Louder." He thrust in to the base, and she cried out. "Like that," he muttered into her hair, littering kisses there. "Just like that, Lola." He said her name with such affection that she momentarily forgot how he was overcoming her. He undid the hooks of her corset, one at a time down her spine. He opened it, smoothing his wide, rough hands over her skin.

"I want it, Beau," she said. "Don't make me wait anymore."

He cleared the hair from her back and buried his face into the crook of her neck. He moved in and out of her slowly. "This is for you," he said.

Everything in her was building, rioting, begging for it. His rhythm never broke, and each stroke of his cock inside her was deliberate. It had such certain purpose— break her piece by piece.

His breath stuttered against her while whispering

how soft, hot, pliant she was. Each word from his mouth was sharper than the last until finally he said, "Now it's for me."

He pounded into her, pulling her head back by her hair until her roots screamed. His lips stubbornly attached to hers from the side as he took her mouth. His other arm wrapped around her shoulders and he became even more merciless until—

"Don't stop," she almost sobbed when he pulled out.

"Turn over."

She flipped onto her back. He towered over her, a force of strength and power. There was no vulnerability in his nakedness. Her shoes were tossed aside. He rounded the bed to the other side as she watched with her head tilted back. He slid her across the mattress by her armpits until her head hung over the edge.

"Is your mouth as hot as your pussy?" he asked, cupping his hands under her head.

She opened immediately for him. He fed her firmly but gently, his forearms flexing as he maintained control, then tightening as he lost it and thrust all the way in. She could only leave her mouth open for his use and hang onto the bedspread as she writhed with the need to come. He pulled out and pushed her breasts together, squeezing his cock between them and fucking her that way.

"Is there any part of you that isn't perfect?" He slipped against her skin easily, wet from her saliva. "You fit right into my hands." He pressed her into the bed as he went harder. "If I'm not careful, I'll come all over you. Would you like that?"

"Yes, Beau," she said.

"Christ, you're sweet." He released her. "Get up. Tell me what you want."

She climbed off the bed and stood in nothing but her stockings. Her clit radiated heat, burning her up from the inside out. "I just want to come," she said shakily.

"There are lots of ways to get there, though," he said, stroking himself as he looked at her. "If you want me to decide, I will."

She nodded hard. "I'm yours."

"Hmm." He circled around her, stopping at her back. He wedged his fingers against her asshole. "I could finish you this way. Have you ever come with a dick in your ass?"

"No," she rasped.

If ever there were a moment she would agree to it, it would be that one, but he let go and said, "I'm far too impatient to break you in right now."

"I want to see your face when you come," she said.

He wrapped his arms around her from behind and kissed her neck. "Then ride me," he said into her ear.

She turned in his arms and pushed his chest. He sat back on the bed. She put her knees on both sides of his hips and held him with one hand as she sank down. "How's that?" she asked coyly.

"You're too far," he groaned.

"I'm as close as I can get."

"No, you aren't."

She bent forward and put her lips to his, creating a

curtain around them with her hair. He angled up to kiss her. She circled her hips over him. Their mouths became hungrier, and he sat up to bury both his hands in her hair.

"Not a day's gone by these past two weeks that I didn't imagine your legs around me," he said.

She lifted herself up to free her legs and wrap them around his back. With her arms circling his neck, she was as close as she could get.

"Dance for me," he said.

"I already did. Now I'm fucking you."

He released her head to clutch her hips and slow her rhythm. "Like this," he muttered. "Dance for me, with me, around me. But do it slow. Savor what you devour."

He slid his hands to the center of her back and pushed her breast into his mouth. He moved from one nipple to the other, sucking on her as she danced herself into a fiery orgasm that consumed everything in its path.

He flipped her onto her back and took what he needed as she tried to keep up with every overwhelming sensation. His muscular arms propped him up, the tendons in his neck strained, his eyes stayed on her bouncing tits until finally he slammed one, two, three times and came deep inside her.

Lola was slick everywhere. She couldn't take her eyes off him as their bodies heaved. A sweat rivulet trickled down his temple onto her stomach. He held himself up with one hand and put the other just above her mound. He circled his thumb once over her pulsating clit. "I want to feel you clench around me again, nice and slow this time."

Her back arched from the mattress. "Ah," she breathed. She was sensitive, but he was gentle—until she was so hungry for her orgasm that she needed it a little harder. She raised her hips, and he increased his pressure, using only his thumb as the rest of his fingers splayed and pressed down on her lower stomach.

He slid in and out of her only a little. "Just to feel my cum inside you," he said lustily. His heavy-lidded eyes didn't leave her face. She tried to tell him it was the most erotic moment of her life, but her words came out as gasps. His arm began to shake from holding himself up, but he didn't stop. Her orgasm seemed to return rather than start again. It roiled through her, slower, deeper, with her hanging onto his cock in a way that made him moan along with her.

His arm gave out, and he collapsed over her. He nuzzled into her neck, kissed her hairline. "Salty," he murmured. "I can't wait to find out how you taste everywhere else."

Lola was ravaged. She welcomed his weight on her already sinking body. She descended limb by limb into the mattress while her mind floated into darkness. Her entire body jerked as she gasped and opened her eyes. "Oh my God," she said. "Did I fall asleep?"

He lifted his head and chuckled. "Just for a second."

"I'm sorry."

"Sorry?"

"I assumed it…wasn't allowed. Sleeping. I thought you wouldn't want to."

He kissed her forehead, her temple. "I don't," he said into her ear.

Her stomach growled.

His body shook on top of her in a silent laugh. "Hungry?"

"Any chance there's actual food on that cart?"

"I can order up something."

"It has to be two in the morning by now."

"For what I'm paying a night, they'll bring us food at any time."

"Mind if I shower while we wait?" she asked.

"I mind."

She wrinkled her nose. "But I'm—"

"Exactly how I want you," he finished. He pulled out from between her legs and fell back on the bed. She turned onto her side. He wrapped one arm around her shoulders and kept her close as he reached for the phone and pulled it to his ear.

"I'd like to order breakfast," he said and paused. "I don't care what time it starts. Send up whatever you have. Omelets, bacon, croissants, orange juice."

"French toast," Lola whispered.

He pulled the phone away. "What?"

"French toast," she said, looking back at him.

"And two orders of French toast." A beat passed before he said, "Well, perhaps tomorrow night I should find a hotel that *can*." He winked at her as he listened. "Ah, I'm so glad you'll make it work."

"Coffee," she added.

"Most importantly, I'll need some coffee too. Yes, that's fine." He hung up and hugged her from behind with both arms. "So she likes French toast."

"As a rule, anything breakfast food."

"Well. I'm glad we get to eat breakfast together." He looked down at her. "But apparently you aren't. You're frowning."

"Sorry," she said quietly.

He rubbed his stubbled chin against her neck, and she smiled. "Good thing you tickle easily."

"I do not," she said, but when he went to do it again, she wriggled in his arms and cried, "Okay, okay, I do."

"So, why the frown?" he asked.

She sighed. "Eating breakfast together almost seems…"

"Worse?" he asked.

"Sounds stupid, doesn't it?"

He leaned in and whispered, "Just think of it as fuel."

"Beau," she chastised, but she was smiling.

"All I can think of when I'm near you is how to get closer."

"You're practically on top of me. You just fucked my tits for God's sake."

He nipped her earlobe. "And you just turned me to stone again with one sentence."

"Already?" Lola asked.

"I've wasted enough time, don't you think?"

"Room service will be here any minute."

"Then we'd better be quick."

He rolled her over and lay on top of her. He swept his hands over her hairline and his lips over her nose

191

and mouth.

"This isn't quick," Lola said, but her sentence ended in a sharp gasp.

He'd reached down and slid his fingers into her. "Just let me appreciate you. That sound you make." He kissed her neck. "The way you feel in my hand," he said against her skin. "That birthmark above your hipbone."

It seemed her mind had turned to mush—she could only answer him in moans. *But you barely know me*, she meant to say. She put her arms around his back.

"Could you see yourself with me?" he whispered, as if someone might hear. He kept stroking her.

"Don't." She closed her eyes. Her voice sounded far away. "Not right now."

"Right now," he countered. "You can't lie when I'm inside you."

When she swallowed, she did it quietly, even though Beau could see her throat. "I don't even know what you're like."

"I'll tell you. Morning is my favorite time of day because it's quiet and no one needs anything from me. So I wake up early and either use the gym or run in the Hills where I live. At work I mostly meet with investors or founders or wherever my secretary sends me. Some nights, more than I'd like, I attend events or parties. Other nights I come home and work more, which I prefer. I don't get a lot of time alone at the office."

Lola had been looking between his and his mouth as he spoke, but her mind was spending the day with Beau. In a way, the complicated life she'd imagined he'd have was even simpler than hers. There was no emotion in his routine, and that made it too easy to stay detached.

"I could ease up on the work," he added as an afterthought. "I've just never had a reason to."

Lola dropped her gaze to his neck. That life didn't appeal to her, but Beau did. Those early-morning or late-night moments when they could intertwine like they were now. He needed that. She didn't. She already had it. Johnny and Beau were miles apart, but even so, one person's taste couldn't be so divided. *Lola* and Beau were miles apart.

"Maybe if things were different," she said. "But they're not."

"Like what? Give me one reason aside from the obvious one."

"The obvious one is a pretty big one," she said. "But okay. I sleep until around noon, so…"

He chuckled. "That's easy. Get a job with regular hours. I'd help you find the right thing. Next?"

"Next?" she asked. "That big reason. Johnny."

He tilted his head at her. "You really think he's the one you're meant to be with?"

She bit her lip when he crooked his fingers inside her and massaged. "I don't believe there's only one person out there for each of us."

"You'll change your mind when I go down on you."

She laughed breathily. "I don't even know what that means."

"It means…I'm confident we'll find that my mouth is made for your pussy." He flashed her a smile. "You'll see. They're meant to be."

"Don't be ridiculous," she said, also grinning.

"Ah, Lola. I don't know what's better, your eyes or your smile."

"You don't have to seduce me," she said. "I'm already in your bed."

"I have to say," he pulled his fingers out and slid them all over her, "I like having you in my bed."

"It's not, though…" The ache in her built again, spurred on by his fingers. "Not your bed. Why would you stay here again tomorrow night?"

"What makes you think I am?"

"You said on the phone."

"Ah," he said. "I just like to get out of my house sometimes."

Her bullshit radar went off. It wasn't even a decent lie. "You're bringing someone else here," she guessed. The words came out sour. Not all of what they'd just done was pretty. Some of it was crude, but those were the moments Lola had submitted completely. Because nobody else could do those things to her that way and make them so good she could've screamed. Her mind flitted between the bedspread underneath her, the mouth above her, the warmth surrounding her. Could he so easily turn around and share that with someone else? She couldn't. "I don't want you to," she said abruptly and unprompted. "I don't want you to do these same things to someone else right after I was here."

"I'm not bringing anyone else here," he said, but it felt as if he was placating her. "Hey."

She'd been staring down again, avoiding him.

"Don't look like that," he said. "It's the truth."

She lifted her eyes again. She was ridiculous for letting her mind go there. It wasn't like her to act jealous. "Okay. Sorry."

"You know what I liked tonight?" he asked. "You on that stage. Asking me to send those women away. I lost it after that. God, you were sexy on that pole. Where'd you learn to dance?"

He was still coaxing her, not enough to get her off, but enough to charm words out of her. She was tempted to tell him the truth—*I used to take off my clothes for money.* There was the risk he might see her differently, though. She didn't want that for the little time they had left. "Ballet," she said.

"Ballet?"

"Classes." She moaned. "In middle school, I took a year of ballet, and we had this…this…," she swallowed, "teacher…"

"Yes?"

She breathed in and out. "I can't think when you're touching me like this."

He stopped but didn't remove his hand. "Your ballet teacher," he prompted.

"She thought I had potential. She took me under her wing. For years after, she let me attend lessons for free. Since I couldn't—Beau, this is worse. Either do it or don't."

He smiled and narrowed his eyes on her. He traced his finger along the outside of her and slipped it inside again.

"She gave me free lessons because I couldn't," her

voice pitched, "afford them."

"A ballerina," he said reverentially. "So she loves to dance."

"She loves to dance." Lola nodded and cocked her head. "I think I heard something."

"Impossible," Beau said. "I just called downstairs."

There was a knock at the door. "Guess they don't have a lot of orders this time of night," she said.

"Ignore it. They'll wait."

She laughed lightly. "You practically threatened their lives if they didn't bring you your breakfast."

He sighed. "Then I guess we'll have to pick this up later." He got up and pulled on his boxer briefs. Lola unpeeled her stockings, found a robe in the bathroom, slipped into it and went out just as Beau was signing the receipt.

He shut the door and turned. "My robe on you," he said, shaking his head slowly, "an image that'll soothe me on my deathbed."

"I was indecent."

He wrapped his arms around her waist. "You were very indecent. But seeing you dressed just makes me want to undress you." He backed her up against the wall and nibbled her neck.

"The food," she said breathily but laughing.

"I'm not hungry."

"Beau," she whined.

"Ah, fuck. Fine." He released her but not before kissing her once on the lips. "First, we refuel."

Chapter Twelve

Beau moved breakfast plates from the food cart to the hotel room's dining table while Lola watched. He distributed silverware and poured them each orange juice. Seated with a napkin on his lap, he drizzled syrup onto his French toast. He cut four bite-sized squares with his fork and knife before looking up at Lola. "Lose your appetite?"

"No."

Earlier, on her way to the bathroom to change into a robe, she'd paused at the closet. Beau's suit had been hung. It'd been done haphazardly, but it was on a hanger nonetheless. There'd barely even been a moment to do it. She'd been faced away from him when he'd taken it off—had he hung it then? It was turning out that the bedroom was the only place Beau could get dirty.

Lola tended toward tidy, but not at that level. She hadn't forgotten Beau's description of his daily routine and as he took a bite of his portioned food, she envisioned him eating that way every morning, alone in a spotless kitchen.

She picked up her French toast, loaded the plate with bacon and fruit and stuck a fork between her teeth. With her other hand, she put the syrup under her arm, picked up a bowl of powdered sugar, turned and walked away.

"Where are you going?" he called after her.

"Eating in bed," she said between her teeth.

He followed her. "You'll make a mess."

She put everything down on the white comforter.

"You already got syrup on my robe," he said, pointing at the sleeve.

"So what? Don't you get maid service?"

"Well, yes. We aren't finished with the bed, though."

She forked an entire half of toast and tore off a bite with her teeth. "So we get a little sticky," she said, chewing. "A little sugary. That so bad?"

He raised both eyebrows at her.

"You ever heard of breakfast in bed?" she asked.

"I don't think this is what's meant by it."

She waved her hand. "Sure it is."

Lola didn't eat breakfast anywhere other than her kitchen, but Beau needed his boundaries pushed a little. She'd crawled on the floor for him—he could handle some unscheduled fun. She took another bite as they stared each other down. When he still hadn't moved, she hopped up on the mattress.

"Lola, what—? Watch the syrup."

"Does this bother you?" she asked, jumping once. The syrup tipped over.

He lunged forward and caught it before more than a few drops escaped. "I just don't understand why—"

She grabbed the syrup from his hands and stuck a finger in it. She glossed some over her lips. "Ready for me?" she asked.

"What—"

She threw her arms around his neck. He caught her just as her legs went around his waist. She kissed him hard on the mouth, spreading syrup all over him.

"What's gotten into you?" he asked.

He'd gotten into her. She wasn't just testing him— she was actually giddy, experiencing a second wind for the night. She licked the sauce from his upper lip. "Hmm. Interesting. There's syrup all over your face, my face, your robe, the bed. And yet, we're still standing."

"Well, *I'm* standing," he said, grinning. "You're just wrapped around me being silly."

She nodded. "Is silly okay?"

"Silly is okay."

"So then come have breakfast in bed with me."

"If you insist, though I don't really see the point."

"There's no point. This isn't a negotiation or a board meeting where there needs to be an explanation for everything. There's absolutely no fucking point at all, and that is the point."

He shook his head. "Fine. We'll eat in bed, but you'll have to get down."

"Take me with you." She twisted to set the syrup back on the bed. "You might need extra hands."

He laughed but adjusted her ass and walked them to the table. She took both glasses of orange juice while he supported her with one hand and carried his plate in the other.

When he lowered her onto the bed with one arm, the powdered sugar teetered. They looked at each other and smiled.

"I feel like a child," Beau said once they were seated and eating. "Even more like a child than when I was a child."

She smiled with her mouth shut as she chewed. "Me too," she said when she'd swallowed.

He took a bite and glanced up. "Why are you looking at me that way?" His legs were crossed in front of him. His forehead wrinkled.

"I'm trying to picture you as a kid," she said. "It's hard. You have a very serious way about you."

"Is serious okay?"

"Well…" She pretended to think. He tore off a piece of bacon and threw it at her. It felt like progress. "Serious is okay," she relented, smiling. "But kids shouldn't be too serious."

"I was responsible," he said. "My dad was not reliable, and he'd leave for periods of time. I kind of became the man of the house."

"You said he was French? Did you ever live there?"

"For a summer when I was seventeen. He went there on one of his stints and God knows why, but I asked to go with him."

Lola put down her fork. "I had the impression you grew up without much—like me."

"I did. He was an artist, and he insisted he couldn't work in America, so he'd go back to France when he could. My mom didn't travel. She'd get on his case so he'd pick up a job for a few months, but he could never keep it. Basically we lived on her secretary's salary."

"He must've really loved you guys to keep coming back when he didn't want to be here."

Beau looked up from his plate. "I ask myself that a lot. Why he even bothered coming back." He cleared his throat.

"He probably missed you," Lola said, chewing. "It's nice to be missed." Her heart sank as she said it. She was probably being missed that very moment. She had to look away from Beau, who was the reason she hadn't been missing Johnny as much as she'd thought she would.

"Have you been to Paris?" he asked, calling her back.

"No," she said. "Vegas is the farthest I've been from here."

"Perhaps a trip is in order." He drank his orange juice, looking at her over the rim of the glass.

She shrugged. "Not right now. This is a chance for us to turn things around."

"Us?" he asked, furrowing his brow. "Me?"

"No, me and Johnny. Owning our own business is a lot of responsibility, and I don't want to mess it up. I—" She paused at the shadowy look in his eyes. "What?"

"I've already told you," he said. "Tonight is about you and me only. If I were your boyfriend, would you keep bringing up your ex?"

"I just thought since we were—"

"The rules haven't changed just because we screwed."

Lola's mouth fell open. It was as if a switch had been flipped from a few minutes earlier when they'd been as playful as two new lovers. "Do you realize how you sound?"

"Inform me," he invited with a gesture of his fork. "Please."

"Like I'm your puppet or something. I don't think I've ever met anyone so controlling."

He shrugged. "You didn't seem to mind my control earlier. In fact…I think you said it was *not repulsive.*"

Lola stood from the bed and crossed her arms.

He looked up. "What?"

"Don't throw my honesty in my face like that. Do you think that was easy for me to say? That I enjoy being with someone other than—"

"Don't you dare say his name," he said, setting down his silverware.

"I'm sorry, Master," she said. She was pushing him, and from the look on his face, he didn't like it. She was too worked up to care. "Why don't you just go ahead and tell me what I should say."

"Is it too much to ask that you don't talk about your boyfriend when you're here with me?" His body locked up as his spine straightened.

"Fine. I won't talk about him." She instinctively took a step back. "Doesn't mean I won't be thinking about him."

"Now you're deliberately testing me. I don't want you talking about him, and I *certainly* don't want you thinking about him while you're in *my* bed."

She pointed a finger at him. "You think money gives you the right to do anything. You pay me, and I'll do whatever you say. You know what, though? You can't control my thoughts."

His face closed, just as she'd expected would happen if she threatened his control.

"How does that make you feel?" she prodded.

He got up from the bed. "Lola, I'm trying to be patient—"

"Muzzle me all you want," she muttered, moving to walk around him, "but there's nothing you can do to stop me from thinking about him when I'm with you."

"Where are you going?"

"I need a minute."

He blocked her with his entire body. "You don't get minutes unless I give them to you. Understand?"

She bolted to the right, but he caught her waist from behind and lifted her. They struggled against each other until Beau had her front pinned up against the window. He grabbed at the lapels of her robe, pulling it open and pressing her bare breasts up to the shockingly cold glass. One hand went over her mouth. He pushed his pelvis into her so her hipbones met the window.

"Take it back," he said in her ear.

Cityscape lights poked holes in the night. Her back was warm with Beau's heat, but her nipples hardened with a chill. She whimpered, unable to speak.

"If I take my hand away, not another fucking

203

mention of him unless *I* bring it up."

She nodded. He released just her face.

"People might see us," she said, ashamed by the obvious thrill in her voice.

"I don't give a fuck." He pushed up the fabric of her robe and entered her from behind.

She moaned, so completely filled with him.

He stilled. "Tell me the truth. Were you thinking of him earlier?"

She gritted her teeth. As if she could think of anything else when Beau had her where he wanted her.

He thrust once. She braced herself against the window with her palms. He grabbed her wrists and held them there as he slid in and out quickly, impatiently. "I'm going to bend you over and spank you so fucking hard if you don't answer." It was not an empty threat. Before she could even begin to formulate a response, he let go of one of her arms and slapped her ass.

"What are you doing?" she cried. It was a slap intended to punish her, and that made her thighs quiver outside her control. She was going to come already.

"Answer me, or I'll turn that sweet, white ass flaming red, Lola. Tell me the truth."

She sucked in a breath. The threat did nothing but make her wildly hot. "What do you want me to—? I-I love him—"

He smacked her again, harder this time, with a swift, delicious sting, right on the outside curve of her behind.

"I didn't think of him," she confessed in one heated gasp. "I couldn't. When you're inside me, there's nothing else."

"Good girl." He seized her wrists again to brace both him and her. The glass rattled under her body as he took her. "You think that was controlling?" he asked between thrusts. "You don't know the half of it. I want to lock you up in this room, feed you and fuck you on my schedule. Then you'd really be mine." He wrapped his hand around her throat to keep her from looking anywhere but outside. "Give them a show, ma chatte. Don't be shy." He released her face to massage her clit.

She pressed her cheek against the window, fogging the glass. "Right there," she said. Her fingers curled into fists. "I'm going to come."

He pulled out and stepped back. "Not yet."

"Please." She dropped to her knees and put her hand between her legs.

"Don't," he said, looming over her. "Do not make yourself come."

"I'm not," she said. "I'm trying to stop it."

"*Stop it?*" He looked incredulous.

"I want you to do it."

"Ah." He smiled and backed away. "You're good. Very good." He took a strawberry from the cart. "Will you come to me?"

She crawled along the floor, hobbling because of the persistent ache between her legs. She let him feed her the strawberry. He bent over and sucked the sweetness from her lips.

"Now lie on your back and bend your knees," he whispered into her mouth.

It was a command that she obeyed without

hesitation.

"Wider," he said.

She bared herself to him.

"Reach up…"

She felt behind her head and grabbed the bedpost with both hands.

"That's it," he said. "Hold on to that."

"You treat me like a dog," she said, but even she heard her own panting.

"And your obedience deserves a reward. Don't you want to know what it is?"

She salivated. There was nothing in her world except him, large and naked, hovering over her. "Yes, Beau."

He squatted and trailed a finger down her stomach and over her pubic bone. His knuckles brushed the inside of her thigh as he traced the outline of her. "You're trembling," he said. "Ask for what you want."

"Touch me," she said softly.

"I already am."

"Lower."

He put his hand on her knee. "Here?"

"Higher."

He slid his hand to the crease of her ass. "You mean here."

"No," she whispered. "Higher."

"You'll have to be more specific."

"My pussy," she said.

He smiled. "I would love to touch your pussy."

Lola's chest rose with exaggerated breaths.

"What should I touch it with?" he asked.

Her eyelids fluttered. "What do you mean?"

He wet his finger and circled it around her opening while she strained to see. "This?" He waited until she looked up at him again. "Or something else?"

"That," she said. "Your mouth."

He ran his hands up her thighs to hold her knees, pushing them apart as wide as they'd go. He returned his hands between her legs, parting her lips with this thumbs. Her back arched, sending her breasts toward the ceiling.

"Perfect," he said. "Just stay that way."

He got on the floor with her. His arms curled around her hips to secure her to his face right as he sucked her into his mouth, thrusting his tongue inside her. Her spine felt as if it would snap in half if she bowed it any more.

"Now I know," he said. "This is what I've been hungry for all along."

She reached down to touch his hair, but he caught her wrist and pushed it back toward her. "Use your words, ma chatte. It makes me hard just hearing your voice."

She gripped the bedpost again. "That," she said when the tip of his tongue massaged her clit. "Keep doing that."

He kept doing that, and when she was close, he moaned with his mouth buried in her. It felt like a crack in his shell, that sound, as it sent vibrations up her body.

"You're right," he spoke without moving away, "mouth is so much better."

She came. His voice was always deep and solid, and

it made the words themselves unexpectedly sensual. They had ways of destroying her control. He continued kissing between her legs until she'd finished.

"How's that?" he asked, his lips running a gentle course along the inside of her thigh.

"Do you have to ask? I'm consumed."

"So am I." He took her waist in his wandering hands and squeezed her. "I could enjoy you for hours. Days. I think maybe we should get some rest, though."

She released the post and got up on her elbows. "Rest?"

"We have a couple hours or so left. Don't worry, I won't oversleep."

"It's not that," she said. As fast as he'd taken her against the window, he hadn't finished. "Don't you…?"

"Don't I what?"

She looked away. What did she care if he was satisfied? It wasn't a requirement of their deal. "Nothing," she said. "Sleep is fine."

"Good." He got to his feet and helped her up. He piled all the dishes from their breakfast onto the food cart and tossed oversized pillows aside. They hadn't even gotten to the sheets yet.

"Are you sure this is what you want?" she asked tentatively. For a savvy businessman, he hadn't used his hours very wisely. It was hard to believe after all the stress she'd endured making the decision that the night was almost over.

"The only thing I want more," he said, getting into the bed without looking at her, "is to smash the alarm clock with my fist. But I can't. Just let me have this."

There was an empty ache where her heart should be. Should be, because only a heartless person could resist Beau in that moment. Should be, because her heart didn't belong in this bed. She climbed right into his arms and curled up to his warmth.

He turned out the bedside lamp. "If I hadn't worn you out, we could've used this time to talk some more," he said. "I would've liked that."

Her eyes were already closed and he said nothing else, so she gave in to the heady feeling of his arms around her and slept.

Chapter Thirteen

Her name and a kiss. And again, her name, clearer, a kiss, firmer. Their bedroom was colder than usual, but it made the bed a haven of warmth. It was dead-of-night quiet. She was being squeezed from behind with a strength and intensity she wasn't used to. All at once she remembered where she was and opened her eyes.

"Lola," Beau whispered. He moved her hair from her forehead. "It's time."

The room was dark except for the boxed, green numbers on the digital clock. Through the large window, black was seeping from the sky, leaving rich sapphire in its place.

"I need to shower," she said. Beau was present everywhere on her body.

He stroked her jaw. She raised her chin to kiss him. She was exhausted and made no effort to hide the fact that she wanted that kiss. He rolled on top of her in one motion and her legs opened for him. He didn't enter her right away, but kissed everywhere above her neck his lips could reach. He pressed himself against her thigh, close enough she could almost feel him inside her.

"I'm ready," she whispered.

He thrust into her and groaned as if he'd been waiting to do it all night. They got slow and quiet, waking up together.

It was good. Too good. She felt him—*him*, not fast and hard and mind-blowing, but satisfying and warm. This slow, sleepy fuck was no less passionate than it'd been against the window. His groans came from somewhere deep inside. It was good—but it was dangerous. When she caught herself clutching him, digging her nails into his back, she stopped and squeezed her eyes shut. "I can't," she said.

"Okay." He kissed her cheek, her nose. "It's okay."

He held her head. It was too dark to see his expression. It meant she could imagine he was Johnny and remove some of the guilt she struggled with. She didn't. Even this way, in the pre-dawn, with his lovemaking, Beau demanded all of her.

As he came, he dropped his face into the crook of her shoulder and gripped her scalp. Then he exhaled what sounded like everything in his lungs. His body loosened on top of her. She stared up at the ceiling. Her limbs, depressed in the mattress, tingled. "I can't feel anything."

"I'm crushing you," he said but didn't move.

"It's not that," she said. Dread had seeped through her in seconds, numbing everything it touched. Her body was in survival mode. Facing Johnny would be as impossible as pretending the night had never happened. Neither thing could be avoided, though. She had to face him. Then they'd have to move on with their lives.

Beau raised his head and opened his mouth. If he asked her not to leave, she didn't know what she'd say. Of course she'd say no. It didn't matter that she wasn't ready to go, or that she was leaving with more questions than she came with. Aside from the confusing fact that she'd actually enjoyed her time with Beau, she realized she'd never see him again after this. She had no reason to. Even if she admitted she wanted to, she couldn't.

He spoke. "We should go. You can't be late."

There was an important detail she'd forgotten for a moment, but when it returned, it overpowered everything else. "I need to shower."

He pulled out of her and pushed the covers back as he got out of the bed. "There's no time."

Her body coiled. She could not walk into Johnny's home this way. "I have to shower," she repeated.

"You can't." He put on his boxer briefs and disappeared into the walk-in closet. "I'm already worried about traffic," he called. "If we don't leave now—"

"Johnny will understand if we're a few minutes late if it means I get to shower."

"No," Beau said firmly. He tossed a shopping bag onto the bed. "This isn't up for discussion. I've never broken the terms of a contract in my life."

Lola sat up, grasping the sheet to her chest. Any numbness dissipated in her panic. "You can't be serious." She dumped out the contents of the bag—the jeans, T-shirt and underwear she'd left her apartment in.

213

"But I'm—I can't go home like this. I'm disgusting."

"Then you should've thought of that earlier. I'm not kidding, Lola. Get up. *Now*."

He was already dressed in a hoodie and jeans, standing with his back straight and his hands on his hips. His hair was messy from sleep, something she would've found cute if anger wasn't rising up her chest. She choked on her words. "C-can't I at least—"

"What aren't you understanding? The sky is already light. Get dressed, or I'll do it for you."

She clamped her mouth shut. What a fool she'd been to want to stay. Beau had been fire and ice all night, his moods swinging higher and further apart each time. "Then turn around," she snapped. "I don't want you to watch."

He shook his head. "Time's almost up, but not quite. You still belong to me."

She swallowed thickly and let the sheet drop. She hooked herself into her bra and tugged her shirt over her head. He looked at his watch. She got out of the bed.

"I have to say," he said thoughtfully as she pulled on her underwear, "this went even better than I imagined."

There was something in Beau's voice Lola didn't recognize. The hair on the back of her neck bristled. "What did?"

"Buying a person."

She stopped moving and looked at him. The shift from who he'd been in bed to the stranger standing in front of her had required less effort than a deep breath.

"You didn't buy 'a person.' You bought a body." She didn't want to be either to him, a person or a body. She wanted to be Lola—the girl he'd seduced over darts, the image that would soothe him on his deathbed. "There's a difference."

"I'm not debating this with you again. There's no difference."

He was so smug, without any trace of the Beau she'd gotten to know. He should've used her like he'd said he would. No talk of family, of possibility. Of her in his life. Anything more than using her body was a kind of cruel that went beyond the boundaries of normalcy. "I hate you," she said. It had come out slippery and unintentional, but she didn't take it back. In that moment, it was true.

"Fine," he said. "But I bought you fair and square. Say it."

"You did *not*," she said. "I am not my body. I am feelings, a brain, a heart. There's so much more to me than what you got."

Beau was gripping his hips so hard, his knuckles were white. She looked away and buttoned her jeans, trying to hide the fact that he'd hurt her.

"You can't just change the terms of an agreement, Lola. Business doesn't work that way."

"This isn't business," she said. "I'm a human being. I didn't sign over my heart to you. You have no right to say you owned anything other than my body."

"Are you saying none of it was real? That your heart wasn't in it?"

"It was real for me, Beau. But it takes a lot

goddamn more to earn someone's heart. You can't expect that in one night, and you damn well can't demand it."

"Enough," he snapped. "Now would be a good time to shut your mouth."

She didn't. It fell wide open. "Beau—"

"Just—" He held up both his hands. "Stop. Stop talking."

She grabbed her purse from the bed. "I'm ready," she said, flipping him off as she stormed by him.

They rode the elevator down in silence. When the doors opened, she practically ran outside. It didn't matter. Beau and his long strides were never far behind. She went straight to where Warner waited against a town car.

"I can go alone," she said over her shoulder, knowing Beau would be there.

"I'm coming."

"I don't see why you have to."

He ignored her. "Warner," he said. "Don't waste any time."

"Yes, sir."

Lola opened the car door herself even though Beau reached for it. She ducked inside and slid as far away as she could get from him.

"Lola."

"Don't talk to me." Her voice threatened to quiver, but she forced it steady. "You're a fucking bastard."

He sighed. "You're right. I'm a bastard and an asshole. Such an asshole. I didn't mean what I said up there. I'm sorry."

She jerked her head to him. The words, in their apologetic, defeated tone, sounded wrong coming out of his mouth.

His eyebrows were drawn. "I mean it. I don't know what came over me." He made a face when he swallowed that made him look as if he was in pain. "Lola, you have to understand. This isn't easy for me. We shouldn't have to say goodbye like this. We shouldn't have to say goodbye at all."

Lola's fists uncurled a little. It was all so confusing, except for the fact that she wasn't ready to say goodbye either. Not even when he was an asshole. "I think I understand. Walking away is easier if we're both angry."

"I don't want to end things this way."

"You were pushing me away."

"If you were smart," he said quietly, "you'd let me."

She looked back out the window. "It doesn't matter. This is the end, anyway."

"Not yet. Come back to me, even just for our last few minutes."

It truly was the end. The horizon was orange. She could be what Beau so obviously needed for a few more minutes. At least she had someone waiting at home for her. She turned back and moved across the seat as he angled to face her. "I never expected it to be this good." He stroked her cheek with his thumb, cupping her jaw. "For you to be so beautiful. For this to feel so right." He paused. "For it to be so hard to say goodbye."

Her breath hitched. She took his wrist with both her hands, overcome with need to give him the truth.

"If we'd met earlier, Beau, or if our circumstances were different, I know I could've—"

"Stay another night."

She blinked. "What?"

"Don't go."

"I can't," she said, shaking her head. She removed her hands and held them to her chest. Fantasizing that he'd ask her to stay and experiencing it were two different things. Even if she wanted to with every fiber of her being, which she didn't, because she loved Johnny—she couldn't. It was ridiculous. "You're not serious. No. I can't."

"Would you do it if I didn't pay you?" he asked.

"No."

"Then I'll pay. He gets his money, and I get you. One more night."

"Absolutely not." She turned forward in the seat and looked away. "I need my phone back."

Fabric rustled. The car slowed. She made the mistake of glancing back at him. His hair, still in disarray, alerted her to a new fracture in her heart, because it became a little deeper in that moment.

He held out the phone for her. "Thank you. Even though it wasn't, it still felt like luck having you at all."

She scanned his face, still incredibly handsome despite his lack of sleep, and took her phone. Out the tinted window, the familiar gates of her apartment complex came into view. When the car stopped, she gripped the door handle painfully hard.

"Lola."

Don't look back. Don't look back. She looked back.

"Come here," he said.

She hesitated, then leaned and met him halfway. He put a hand on her cheek to hold her there. "I have my flaws. I don't deserve a yes from you," he said. "There's more to you than one night, though, and there's more to me. He can have the money. We can have the rest of each other." He kissed her. "I won't change my mind. You know how to reach me." He let her go and turned back to his window.

She stepped out onto the sidewalk. The car pulled away from the curb. Her feet had walked this path thousands of times—they knew the way home on their own. She willed them to move. Going home was the right thing to do. She and Johnny were forever altered, but he was waiting for her.

The car braked at a stop sign a second too long, and her breath caught.

The price of a million dollars was not her body. It was glimpsing what could've been and wondering for the rest of her life if she should've been in that car. It was the seed of doubt planted in her mind that could potentially grow many different branches.

The car turned and drove away. She glanced over her shoulder. She was out of time. The sun was just beginning to rise over the city.

BOOKS IN THE

Explicitly Yours Series

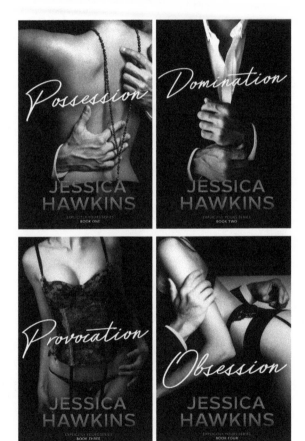

TITLES BY
JESSICA HAWKINS

LEARN MORE AT JESSICAHAWKINS.NET/BOOKS

SLIP OF THE TONGUE
THE FIRST TASTE
YOURS TO BARE

THE CITYSCAPE SERIES

COME UNDONE
COME ALIVE
COME TOGETHER

EXPLICITLY YOURS SERIES

POSSESSION
DOMINATION
PROVOCATION
OBSESSION

STRICTLY OFF LIMITS

ABOUT THE AUTHOR

JESSICA HAWKINS grew up between the purple mountains and under the endless sun of Palm Springs, California. She studied international business at Arizona State University and has also lived in Costa Rica and New York City. To her, the most intriguing fiction is forbidden, and that's what you'll find in her stories. Currently, she resides wherever her head lands, which is often the unexpected (but warm) keyboard of her trusty MacBook.

CONNECT WITH JESSICA

Stay updated & join the
JESSICA HAWKINS Mailing List
www.JESSICAHAWKINS.net/mailing-list

www.amazon.com/author/jessicahawkins
www.facebook.com/jessicahawkinsauthor
twitter: @jess_hawk

CPSIA information can be obtained
at www.ICGtesting.com
Printed in the USA
LVHW040723231118
598036LV00001B/312/P

9 780997 869118